*Life for the travelers on the Oregon Trail*
*is hard, extremely hard.*

As they traveled, they saw more and more graves as well as animal carcasses along the Trail. They also met turnarounds nearly every day. They all told of the same dire future for the wagon train. . .

"I'm hot," Willie said one day. "I need a drink, Martha. Please, get me a drink."

"I can't, Willie. We have to wait until we stop tonight."

"I can't wait. I'm thirsty now."

"So am I," Petey said. "My throat hurts."

"Why don't we pretend we're in a nice cool lake, swimming," Rachel said. "The water comes to our shoulders so we just lie down and start kicking our legs and stroking with our hands. Are you getting too cold, Willie?"

Willie laughed with delight at the game. "Not yet," he said. "I want to swim some more."

"All right," Rachel said. "Just be careful you don't go out too far. It might get deep."

Both boys got into the game until they forgot all about being hot and thirsty. . . .

The next afternoon the train stopped for some reason. . . .When Rachel went to see what was wrong, she found Tom Dorland talking softly to Tamara Richards. As he talked, Rachel realized a snake had bitten the woman.

# HEARTBREAK TRAIL

VeraLee Wiggins

A Barbour Book

*For my most special husband in the world,*
*I appreciate your faithful, caring, gentle way.*
*Encouraging but not pushing; helping but not forcing,*
*And always being there, no matter what my need.*
*I love you more than words can say, Sweetie Pie.*



ISBN 1-55748-991-2



Published by Barbour & Company, Inc.
P.O. Box 719
Uhrichsville, OH 44683
http:\\www.barbourbooks.com

ecpa Member of the Evangelical Christian Publishers Association

Published in the United States of America.

## one
## March 1, 1859

"Papa," Rachel Butler wailed, her blue eyes flashing. As she shook her head in emphasis, tendrils of red hair fell from her neatly done braid and then curled around her plump face. "You don't seriously expect me to go all the way to Oregon! Out there, if the Indians don't get you, the wolves will. Besides I'm all registered to start Illinois College this fall. Please, Papa, take me home!"

"Ha!" Papa said. "You'll learn more in six months on the Oregon Trail than you would in four years of college."

Eighteen-year-old Rachel Butler was an only child who'd had the good life in her home in Quincy, Illinois. Nathan Butler, her father, had earned plenty of money for his family in his successful blacksmith shop.

"It'll take all summer to get to Oregon, Papa, if we don't die on the way. It's not fair to make me miss college because of your senile whim."

Tall, graying Nathan Butler, with his clear blue eyes, wide upturned lips, and straight-as-a-ramrod, trim, muscular body, looked anything but senile. Just having bought three covered wagons, he displayed undiluted excitement. No one in the world could be kinder than this man who'd always been her champion. But forcing her to go to Oregon in a covered wagon? How could he do that to her?

His soft eyes met her angry ones, unflinching. Then they crinkled into a smile. "We're going, Rachel, so why don't you decide to have fun? Don't you know we're making history? Now, go get your mother and let's find the cattle market. We need about fifteen yoke of oxen."

Rachel didn't rush going for her mama, but found her in a fancy dress shop. BOUTIQUE, ELEGANTE—INDEPENDENCE, MISSOURI, the sign above the door said. "Come on," Rachel said quietly, "Papa wants us to help him buy a million oxen."

"Why in the world would he expect us to do that?" Mama asked, hurrying to the shop's door where she almost collided with her husband who'd come seeking her.

His eyes expressed joy at seeing his two "lassies," as he called Alma and Rachel. "What would you be doing in such a fancy place just before starting on the Oregon Trail?"

Alma looked surprised. "Looking for things that won't be available in the wild country."

Nate laughed out loud. "Come on, woman, you won't need anything like those dresses where we're going. Let's go buy some oxen. Should we buy a saddle horse for each of us, too? I'd like to take some milk cows along and a few chickens. I'll bet no one has cows or chickens in Oregon yet."

In the next few days Nate bought the stock he'd suggested plus bolts of sheeting, linsey-woolsey, and denim for men's clothing. Then Nate asked to see the best walking shoes they had.

With disdain Rachel tried on the heavy high-top shoes. "I can't wear these things, Papa," she wailed. "I'd never let anyone see me in them."

"Are they comfortable?" Papa asked.

"Yes, but what good will that do if I don't wear them?"

He nodded with a small smile. "You'll wear them. We'll take three pairs," he said to the storekeeper. While Rachel fussed, he bought three pairs of shoes for Alma and three for himself.

Then Rachel didn't like the warm mittens he bought for each of them. "At least they don't have to be that ugly gray-brown color," she said. "Why can't they be bright?"

"I don't see any others," Papa said. "Wrap them up," he instructed the man.

Then they bought staples: flour, dried beans, dried apples, coffee, sides of bacon, sugar, salt, and baking powder. He bought some potatoes and fresh meat to use the first few days. He added a dutch oven for baking over the fire, some simple pots, and the cheapest of dishes and silverware.

Back at the wagons, Papa put in things he'd brought from home: books, a family Bible, a dictionary, an arithmetic text, a grammar book, some charts, maps, old letters, and diplomas of graduation.

He put some heavy blacksmithing tools into one of the wagons, the only cargo that that wagon carried. In another wagon he put a double-sized featherbed on the wagon floor for him and Alma, two comfortable chairs, plus some of the other things. Rachel's wagon contained one cozy chair, a single-sized featherbed, and the rest of the things they had to take.

"Everything's ready," Papa said, his voice ringing with excitement. "But I have one more thing to do."

Rachel watched with wonder as Papa tore the floorboards from one of the wagons, pushed in a big pouch of money, and replaced the boards. "There," he said, triumphantly, "no one would ever know there's a false floor in that wagon. Would you have known, Rachel?"

She shook her head. "Who cares about false floors anyway?"

He grinned. "You'd better care, lassie! I just put all our extra money in there. Plenty to buy everything we need to get started in Oregon. We'll be leaving in a couple of days, I hope. You know this train we're joining is all

Christian, don't you?"

Rachel shrugged. "I know, Papa. You've told me that before. But I couldn't care less. It isn't like joining a church. We'll just be traveling together for safety. We probably won't even meet the people in the other wagons."

Nate got to his feet and jumped down from the wagon. "You want me to give up on you, Rachel? Let you have a terrible time on this whole trip? Well, I just might do that." He walked over to a group of men standing around talking.

The next day, while Papa and the other men elected a train captain and decided on the rules for the wagon train, Rachel and Mama went on a last walk around town. They found a beautiful green ball gown that set off Rachel's red hair to perfection. "I must have it, Mama," Rachel said, spinning around. "You know I won't find one this perfect in Oregon. Their gowns will probably be made from flour sacks. I doubt they ever heard of satin."

Mama sighed. "I know, love, but Papa told me we can't buy anything more. He says we have to load lightly so the oxen can pull the wagons two thousand miles."

Rachel stomped her slippered foot, but took off the gown. Then the two had a long leisurely dinner at a nice restaurant and returned to the maze of wagons and people. Oxen and cows bawled, horses nickered, people yelled, and children cried. The barnyard smell didn't add much to Rachel's serenity, either.

Somehow Papa spotted them and hurried to them. "Everything's all set," he said. "We leave in the morning at sunrise."

He led them to their wagons and talked to them as he fastened a box containing five chickens to the back of Rachel's wagon. "Now we'll not only have milk, cream, and butter," he said, "but we'll have eggs to go with our bacon." He stopped talking and peered at his lassies. "Can't you be a little excited?" he asked.

Alma patted his forearm. "I'm getting excited, dear. It's going to be fun."

Rachel didn't answer.

Nate took them out for supper. "The last time we eat in a restaurant until we reach Oregon," he said as though bragging.

"How did the meeting go, dear?" Alma asked, putting a bite of dainty white bread into her mouth.

A huge smile spread across Nate's face. "Just fine," he said. "We elected Charles Ransom for captain. He'll be good. Hasn't been over the trail but he's read all he can get hold of. And we decided to use the Ten Commandments for our laws. Ransom said we'd be here the rest of our lives trying to get up as good a set of laws as the Creator gave us." He picked up his knife and fork, cut a bite from his steak, and put it into his mouth. "Oh, yes," he said after eating a few more bites, "Ransom had a bunch of copies of the Latter-day Saint's Emigrants' Guidebook, by Clayton. He said it's by far the best guidebook out so I bought one."

Rachel swallowed her bite of salad. "Who needs a guidebook, Papa? You said the trail is well marked."

Nate laid down his fork and nodded. "Yes. Well, the book doesn't just show where the trail is. It tells about things like camping spots where there's water, grass, and wood, how far we've come and still have to go. And lots of other things we'll need to know. Say, did you know some of the men are riding horses? No wagons?" He thought a second and smiled. "One's riding a cow. This oughtta be some journey, lassie."

When they returned to their wagons, Captain Ransom stood at the next wagon in line, inspecting its load. "You can't haul this much in one wagon," he told the man.

"Them's tried allays wear out their oxen and end up leavin' the stuff beside the road anyways. Better save your animals and lighten the load now."

He left that wagon and approached the Butler wagons. After looking them over, he turned to Nate. "You done good, Butler. You'll get there with as many belongings as anyone, anyways. Might even get there with all your oxen." He started to walk away, then turned back. "For identification, this here wagon train'll be called the Ransom Train."

Papa saluted. "Sounds good to me."

The captain started away but turned back again. "I notice you got a herd of cattle. Got anyone to drive them?"

"Nope. Never gave it a thought."

The grizzled man grinned. "Better give it a couple." He motioned with his thumb over his shoulder. "Some men over there are hopin' to work their way on the Trail." With that, he walked away.

As soon as the captain left, the man in the next wagon approached. "Wha'd the old windbag say to you? Thinks he's God already."

Papa looked at Rachel and winked. "He's purty good. Watchin' out for the animals and all. What you got in that wagon anyway? Seems to have set him off right good."

The man stuck his hand out to Papa. "Thurman Tate. Come'n see what you think."

Rachel followed Papa and Tate to the wagon. She peered inside at a heavy iron cookstove, a big chiffonier, and a heavy dresser. It looked heavenly to her. She'd wanted desperately to bring her beautiful piano but Papa wouldn't hear of it. "Want to kill the oxen?" he'd asked knowing how much Rachel loved animals. They'd ended up leaving the piano as well as her small dog and two cats with her grandmother.

"Ransom's right," Papa told Tate. "You'll kill your animals and lose the stuff, too. Better unload it here whilst you can get somethin' out of it."

"Never," Tate said. "My wife needs that stuff." He gazed at the oxen a moment. "Them's strong animals, ain't they?"

Nate looked the oxen over. "They're strong all right, but they have a two-thousand-mile pull ahead of them. Better give them every advantage you can." He took Rachel's arm and headed back toward his wagon. "Good luck, neighbor," he called but he got no response.

When Rachel climbed back into her wagon, she saw Papa a ways away, talking to a group of men. Probably hiring someone to herd the cattle to Oregon. She lay down on her soft featherbed, thinking. Is there any way at all we can stop Papa from this insane idea? If we really go, we'll probably all die before we get there.

The next morning, March fifteenth, men shouting, oxen bawling, and the smoke and the smell of bacon and coffee cooking awakened Rachel early. . .very early. She hustled into her clothes and climbed down from her wagon. Mama handed her a plate of pancakes, bacon, and eggs, smothered in syrup, and a cup of coffee, black and steaming.

In an hour the wagon masters had yoked the oxen and lined up the wagons in the order they'd travel; the next day, the wagon at the head of the line would move to the back. Rachel climbed into her chair in her wagon. Lots of people milled around on the ground preparing to walk. The atmosphere seemed gala, almost like a big celebration. Well, she'd see how all those silly people felt in a few days. Maybe by then they'd realize what they were getting into.

When the young man beside Rachel's oxen started them

moving, Rachel felt herself jarred, jerked, and jolted. The chickens on the back of her wagon must have felt the same way for they all started squawking.

Twenty-seven wagons, sixty people, a dozen horse riders, and one cow rider began the long ordeal.

Before an hour had passed, Rachel developed a headache as well as a painful back, bottom, and several other body parts. After a few hours, she wondered how she was going to stand such pain every day for six months. Papa had had some crazy ideas in his life, like the time he'd brought home a guitar for her knowing full well that the piano was her instrument. Well, after she got over the shock and took some guitar lessons, she found that she enjoyed it a lot. In fact, her guitar lay tucked among some bedding in her wagon.

But he'd really done it now. Mama must be in agony, too. Then she remembered Mama walking with some women from other wagons. Mama had invited her to walk with them but she wasn't about to walk. Riding was bad enough!

At nooning time Rachel sat on the tongue of the wagon while Mama cooked some potatoes and bacon for lunch. "Here you are," Mama said, cheerfully handing Rachel a heavily laden plate. "That should give you energy for the afternoon."

"Don't you start, too," Rachel growled, shoving in a bite of bacon-flavored potatoes. "Papa's ruined my life. If you switch to his side I won't have anyone left."

Mama tried to put her arm over Rachel's shoulders but Rachel shook it off. "I didn't realize there were sides," Mama said, "but we're on our way so we may as well enjoy it."

"I'm not having fun," Rachel said, "and I'm smart enough to know it. Why don't you go eat so I can at least enjoy my food?"

Rachel thought she'd never survive until evening but she did, hurting in every joint, bone, and muscle. When they stopped for the night, she gingerly climbed down and sat on the wagon's tongue again.

"Come help me with supper," Mama called. "Moving around will make your bones feel better."

Rachel refused. Sitting on the tongue she wondered how she got into this mess and how far they'd go before discovering how dumb it was. Then, hearing squawking, she remembered the poor chickens. Were they the only ones besides her who had sense enough to abhor this trip? She got some cracked corn and water for them and went back to the wagon's tongue feeling a little better.

"Come eat, Rachel," Papa called. "We have fresh butter for our hot biscuits. The churning can worked and Mama's fixed up a grand supper." Rachel still felt grumpy but ate a good meal.

The next morning, Mama awakened Rachel at dawn to eat breakfast. After she finished, she struggled back into the wagon. How could riding in a wagon possibly make a person so horribly sore? How could a bunch of people and animals possibly make so much noise? How could Papa possibly have forced her into this ridiculous pilgrimage?

As Rachel sat there feeling sorry for herself, she saw movement out of the corner of her eye and looked left. A dark-haired young girl ran up beside her wagon. A medium-sized black, gray, and white dog trotted beside her. "Come on down and walk," the girl called. "It's lots easier."

"Why should I walk?" Rachel snapped. "It wasn't my idea to come on this idiotic trek." Rachel watched the girl's shoulders slump and her run slow to a walk.

"Okay. Goodbye then," the girl called and ran ahead,

probably finding someone else to walk with her.

Rachel's conscience bothered her a little for being so rude to the girl who was just trying to be friendly. But why should she care? She couldn't walk with every inch of her hurting so badly, could she? Wondering if she could live through the rest of the afternoon, she changed her position for the five-hundredth time.

Just when she thought she'd scream in agony, she saw a man riding on the back of a small Jersey cow. He looked unstable hanging onto his belongings with one hand while trying to control the cow with the other. The cow looked as if it were about to fall down under the man's weight which was obviously too much for her.

When Rachel's wagon moved ahead of the cow, she realized the man and his cow were falling behind. She leaned forward to watch him when suddenly the cow dropped her rear end sharply. The man tumbled off backwards, his arms pinwheeling in the air. Rid of her burden, the cow took off running with the man ten feet behind her, screaming.

Rachel almost laughed until she remembered where she was and how unhappy she was. How could she even think of laughing out here on this horrendous trail? How could she endure the pain any longer?

Then the dark-haired girl appeared beside the wagon again. This time she had a small blond boy with her as well as the dog. "Come on," she called merrily, apparently having forgotten Rachel's rudeness of the morning. "It's fun to walk," she continued. "I'm walking all the way to Oregon." She giggled happily as if she were having lots of fun. She indicated her dog. "Josephine has to walk. Papa told me that before he let me bring her." She giggled again and shrugged. "So, I have to walk with her. Come on. Even my little brother will walk a lot. Maybe halfway. One reason we walk is that this trip is purely hard on the oxen. Every step we take makes it easier on them."

Rachel hated to give in. After all she couldn't think of a single reason why she should walk. She came on this trip under duress and should make it as easy on herself as possible. On the other hand, she liked animals better than people. So if it would make it easier on the oxen. . . besides, her behind was killing her.

After glancing at the dark-haired girl's cumbersome shoes, she reached into a box and pulled out a pair of her ugly new shoes and put them on. Then she climbed down as the oxen lumbered along with the wagon. No sooner had her feet touched ground than the shaggy dog, Josephine, ran and laid her big head against Rachel's side, stealing her heart. She patted the dog's dirty fur. "Nice girl," Rachel said softly. "Oh, Josephine, you're so sweet and you like me, don't you?"

The dog raised her head and looked deep into Rachel's eyes then gave her one lick on the hand. "I love your dog," Rachel heard herself say. Now why did she do that? Just because she'd climbed out of the wagon hadn't meant she wanted to be the little waif's friend.

"She likes you too," the dark-haired girl said. "She doesn't take to everyone like that. You must be a special person. I'm Martha Lawford. This is my little brother, Willie, and that's Josie you're petting."

Rachel stiffly told Martha her name.

"Oh, aren't you thrilled to get to go to Oregon?" Martha asked, excitement making her voice ring. "I'm just having so much fun already. I can tell it's going to be a good trip."

"Don't be too sure," Rachel grunted.

"But I'm not going to Oregon," Martha said, ignoring Rachel's negative comment. "We're stopping in Walla Walla Valley, in Washington Territory. That's about three hundred miles before Oregon City. Oh, Rachel, I can't wait to see it. My brother, Jackson, says it's God's Garden of Eden on earth."

"I've heard the same thing about the Willamette Valley," Rachel said. "As far as I'm concerned, Quincy, Illinois fits the description just fine."

As the girls continued talking and walking along, the man who'd been riding the cow tore past them still screeching at the cow that was no longer in sight. The girls looked at each other and burst into wild laughter. "I hope he never finds her," Rachel said. "I saw him riding her and she about collapsed under his weight. It was awful."

Rachel walked with Martha again the next day and found it much better than trying to ride. At the end of the second day of travel, the train camped on the Missouri-Kansas border. A festive air emanated from the camp.

"What's all the laughing about?" Rachel asked her mother.

"Everyone thinks we're leaving civilization," Mama said, wearing a happy smile. "I don't exactly know why as Kansas has been a U.S. territory for five years."

Nevertheless, after the meals were finished and cleaned up, someone brought out one of those new-fangled instruments called an accordion, and someone else a violin. Before long, lively music brought the plains to life. Soon, a square dance was being called and danced. Many people stood around, singing the mood-elevating songs.

"Why don't you take your guitar out there and play?" Papa asked.

Rachel wasn't about to enter into such foolishness. Why, they didn't even have a floor under their feet. Just grass and dust. What was there to sing about, anyway? She sat on her usual seat, the wagon's tongue, to wait for the crowd to settle down and to just think. One of the chickens had died that day while they traveled; the others looked bad.

Papa had said they should eat them. He might be right.

"I say, you look lonely," a young man said. "Gotta git up and work out the kinks. Wanna go out there with me?" Not waiting for an answer, he squatted on his heels near Rachel. "I'm Martha Lawford's brother, Jackson."

Why this? Didn't she have enough to put up with? The young man looked clean but his clothes had been mended in several places. Rachel jumped to her feet, elaborately dusting off her long skirt. "I'm afraid I'm tired, Mr. Lawford. If you'll excuse me, I think I'll try to get some sleep, if that's possible with all the racket around here." Then she hopped into the wagon, leaving Mr. Lawford sitting there, alone.

# two

Rachel almost laughed at the man's look of surprise.

"Well, good night, Miss Butler," Jackson Lawford called into the wagon. "I'm sure we'll see each other again."

She heard him plodding across the ground. There. She'd been rude to both Martha and her brother. But what did it matter? They'd never see each other again after this summer. But already she couldn't help liking Martha a lot. Maybe she shouldn't have been rude to Jackson. She could have let him know, without being rude, that she wasn't interested. Oh well, what's done is done.

The next day, Mark Piling's wagon broke an axle. The slight, rough-sounding man with tobacco-stained teeth, was angry and used words that indicated to Rachel he'd forgotten at least temporarily that he was a Christian. No one seemed to know what to do, so Nate Butler hauled out his tools.

"Better call nooning," Nate told Charles Ransom, who was trying to calm the irate Mark Piling. "This'll take a while."

Several young men crowded around Nate, helping however they could. "Looks to me as how that axle was near broke before we started on this here trip," a tall thin man said.

They finished the job in a little less than five hours. "Thanks, fellows," Nate said. "That's the quickest I ever fixed an axle."

Mark Piling didn't thank anyone. "Sandy!" he yelled at his wife, "why aren't you in the wagon and ready to go? I notice you're always in the wagon, sick, when it's time to do a little work." He emphasized the word "sick" as though he doubted it. "Get that boy into the wagon right now. You're holding up the whole train."

The thin pale woman adjusted the baby in her arms and climbed into the wagon with no help from her husband. "Petey," she called weakly, "come on now. We're starting again." A moment later, a little boy showed up from somewhere and silently climbed into the wagon beside his mother and sister.

As the wagons began to move, Rachel, walking with Martha, Martha's little brother, Willie, and Josie, moved close to Martha. "I see everyone isn't all that pleasant on this wonderful 'Christian' wagon train."

Martha laughed quietly. "He prob'ly felt purely awful holding up the train. It's hard for some people to put others out." She grinned at Rachel. "He may truly be the nicest person we could ever meet."

Rachel grunted. Why couldn't Martha have agreed with her? Maybe she didn't like Martha so much after all. She might be a goody two shoes.

Later that afternoon Rachel noticed the man who'd been riding the cow coming toward them from the front of the train, his gray hair flying, mud and dust decorating his torn overalls. "Where's your cow?" she asked impishly.

"Ain't seen that critter for over twenty-four hours now," he ground out. "She'd better stay outa my sight, too. She might make a big barbecue for this here train."

Rachel couldn't stop pestering the man. "How come you're going the wrong way?" she asked. "It's far enough to Oregon without going backwards part way."

"I ain't dumb enough to walk all that way," he grumbled. "I'm goin' back to Independence afore I git any farther away." He jerked his head forward and, with a determined stride, started off toward the back of the train.

"I wish I could go with you," Rachel called after him

but he didn't miss a step. "Guess that means I don't get to go," she muttered.

The next day they came to a stream with a rickety bridge over it. As the first wagon, which happened to be Rachel's that day, approached the bridge, two tall Indians dressed in buckskins and moccasins came to meet the men driving the oxen. The Indians' long black hair hung in single braids down their backs.

"Twenty-five cents to cross," one of them said.

"Not me," Rachel said. "That bridge'll fall down if a wagon tries to cross."

Nate, driving the wagon behind her, came up to see what was going on. When told, he asked the Indians if the water was deep. They assured him it was. Nate pulled out seventy-five cents for his three wagons and they made it across without incident. Soon, the rest of the train crossed too, one wagon at a time.

All except Mark Piling. "I ain't gonna pay them savages nothing," he grumbled. "I'll just walk my critters across."

"Better not," Nate said. "They said the water's deep."

Piling didn't bother to answer but drove his animals to the water and began lashing them when they refused to go in. Finally, after losing several strips of hide to the whip, they gingerly stepped into the stream. When they faltered, he whipped them again until they walked into water up to their bellies. Suddenly, the wagon began to sink.

"Help!" Piling yelled.

Immediately, Nate Butler ran into the river. Upon reaching the oxen, he took hold of their yokes and pulled. "Come on," he said. "You can do it. Come on, boys, pull!" The valiant animals gave it all they had but the wagon didn't move. Several more men, in water to their waists, positioned themselves behind and beside the wagon. "This thing's goin' deeper in the mud every second," one yelled. "We'd best hurry." On the count of three, the men in the back shoved the wagon, those on the sides lifted, while four in the front pulled with the oxen. Their concerted effort unmired the wagon and it then rolled on with the men pushing and pulling with the oxen. In a little more than an hour, the wagon rolled up on the far bank, none the worse for wear. Several men dropped to the grass, gasping for breath.

"Well, I done it," Piling said. "Glad I din't help make them savages rich."

Rachel, who'd been watching the excitement from the bank with Martha, jerked to face her friend. "Did you hear what he said? And not a single man answered him. How come?"

Martha laughed a merry little tinkle. "Because this is a Christian train. Didn't you know?"

Rachel nodded her head. "I know. But what does that have to do with anything?"

"God doesn't want us all to go around saying mean things to each other. Instead, we have to forgive people like Mark Piling."

You might, Rachel thought. But I'm staying clear of that cowboy. I don't like him. I won't forgive him either.

As the wagon train continued, Martha and Rachel had only to stroll to keep up with the slow-moving oxen. Even Willie kept up with no trouble for several hours at a time. And Josie ran circles around everyone.

That day they made camp at noon so everyone could prepare for the Sabbath rest tomorrow. When Rachel fed and watered the chickens, she discovered another dead one. This trip was even harder on the chickens than on her. She felt bad to have them dying. After all they didn't ask to be stuck into a crate and hauled on the bumpy wagon. She dug a hole with Papa's shovel and buried the dead hen.

"Want to learn how to make cakes in the dutch oven?" Mama asked when Rachel returned. "It's a big pot you put over the fire, sort of like an oven. Then you put your cake pan or biscuits into it to bake."

Rachel shook her red head. "No. I don't even know how to make cakes in a real oven. And I don't care to." She walked off to find Martha. But her friend was busy doing her family's washing. Josie greeted Rachel as though she hadn't seen her for days. Rachel sat down in the grass and petted the dog for a while then wandered back to her own wagon.

When she got back, she found Mama doing their washing in cold water from the stream they camped beside. She noticed Mama looked a little tired but she didn't offer to help and Mama didn't ask.

Papa found her sitting on the ground and sat beside her. "The chickens don't look good," he said.

"No."

"They're going to die one at a time, you know."

"I know. Oh, Papa, why did we come on this foolish thing?"

"We came because it was the thing to do. Thousands have made this trip already, Rachel, and are starting new lives in Oregon. One day you'll be glad you came. But, back to the chickens. I think the kindest thing we can do is to prepare them for tomorrow's dinner."

Rachel reluctantly agreed, so that's what he did. At least the chickens were through suffering.

That night a good-looking young man went from wagon to wagon inviting everyone to an evening worship service. When the Butlers arrived, they sat on the grass along with everyone else.

Then the young man stood before the group. Rachel noticed first his broad shoulders and muscular body. Then she saw how tall he stood, well over six feet. His closely clipped dark beard and mustache complemented his longish dark hair and eyes to perfection. She'd never seen a more handsome man anywhere, not even in the big church in Quincy.

"Hello," he said loudly enough for everyone to hear. "I'm James Richards. I believe I'm the only minister on the train so I'll be taking the responsibility of keeping you close to the Lord on this hard trip. Let's begin with some singing."

With his strong baritone voice, he led them in a dozen happy hymns. Soon, nearly everyone joined and the group truly "made a joyful noise unto the Lord." Rachel enjoyed the singing and gladly joined in. Then the young minister preached a short sermon about serving the Lord no matter where you are. "Remember," the handsome young man said, "Daniel served God from the lion's den, and Shadrach, Meshach, and Abednego served from the fiery furnace. I have no doubt we'll think we're in one or the other before we finish this emigration, but we can serve the Lord no matter what's happening or where we are." He closed the meeting with another song and a prayer.

As Rachel walked away, she saw people flocking around Pastor Richards. She wouldn't have minded flocking a little herself. As she lay in her bed that night she decided the trip just possibly might not be so bad after all. Finally, she fell asleep.

Men shouting, oxen bawling, smoke from camp fires, and children crying jerked Rachel from a sound sleep at dawn the next morning. What was this, anyway? She'd expected to sleep late this morning. It was the Sabbath, wasn't it? She turned over on her feather mattress and hoped to fall asleep again, but it wasn't to be. Too many loud voices, too much clattering and banging around. Finally, she struggled from her warm nest, pulled on her clothes, and jumped to the ground to see what was happening.

"The good Lord'll be pleased if you rest with us," Captain Ransom told someone she didn't recognize. "You know the fourth commandment, don't you? Besides, the animals'll fare better with a rest day each week. This trip ain't gonna be easy. Think it over, brother. The good Lord knew what He was doin' when He made the rules for us to live by."

"Well, we're goin'," the strange man said.

"Didn't you know this was a Christian train when you joined?" Ransom asked.

"Shore, but no one said it was fanatical. Might's well save your breath, Captain. We're goin'."

After more noise and confusion, the camp became deathly still but Rachel couldn't fall back to sleep. She lay in bed nearly an hour before jumping up, wide awake.

Mama squatted beside the campfire, cooking breakfast. After greeting Rachel, she hurried to tell her news. "Six wagons left this morning. That leaves twenty-one. Think we'll make it all right?"

Rachel dropped to the ground beside Mama. "Of course. Who needs those people anyway? Who needs anyone?"

Mama smiled sweetly. "I'm sure we all need each other a lot, Rachel. What makes you so caustic this morning?"

"I don't care if everyone leaves, Mama. I really don't. But I do care that those idiots woke me at dawn on the one day I planned to sleep late. I was counting on catching up on my sleep. This is the day of rest isn't it?"

After breakfast the minister gathered his flock again and had a nice long hymn sing, then a prayer meeting in which everyone who wanted to, prayed. Then he preached a sermon about God, living within us wherever we are.

The man impressed Rachel but she disagreed with his message. "I give God credit for being smart," she told Martha as they walked back to their wagons. "And He'd never be dumb enough to come on a fool's trip like this."

Martha looked at her with twinkling eyes. "Don't you know the Lord says in His sacred Word that He'll live in us if we belong to Him. Don't you believe that, Rachel? If you do, you have to know He's with us everywhere, even out here in the prairie."

Whether God was here wasn't high on Rachel's list of things to worry about, so she didn't.

That day the entire wagon train put their food together for a giant potluck dinner. While they ate, Rachel got a chance to see most of the young people on the train. She felt delightfully surprised to learn there were many more young men than women, even though they looked and talked like yokels. If she'd gone to college she'd have had the cream of the crop from which to choose.

She discovered a skinny woman, named Tamara, was Pastor Richards's sister. Unimpressive, the mousey little thing looked like the pastor's shadow, letting him do most of her thinking for her. Rachel felt she and Tamara had nothing in common, but what did it matter? She'd probably never see her again on the Trail or later.

Soon after the meal, Pastor Richards came over to where the girls relaxed on the grass. He folded his long frame and gracefully dropped to the ground beside them.

"How's the weather down here?" he asked. "I've been noticing how comfortable you two looked all afternoon. Now I get to find out for myself."

"Oh, Pastor Richards," Rachel gushed, "I'm so glad you stopped to see us. I may never have heard a better speaker than you. And what a beautiful singing voice. How did we ever get so lucky as to have you on this wagon train?"

"Thank you," he said casually. Then he turned his attention to Martha. "How did you feel about the services?"

She thought a moment. "Well, I purely loved the singing. And I'd never get through a day if God didn't live in my heart. We need Him more out here in the wild than we ever did at home."

He nodded. "Right you are. And how are you enjoying the traveling? Haven't I seen you walking?"

"Oh, yes. My dog, Josie, and I are walking all the way. Now Rachel walks with us and it's lots more fun."

He talked to Martha a few more minutes then hopped to his feet. "So nice talking to you ladies," he said. "And I'm especially glad you're enjoying the journey so much. I'm sure we'll be meeting again. I must get back to my sister. She's shy so she depends on me a lot. Good bye."

As he walked off, Rachel felt herself getting angry. Very angry. She hopped to her feet too, and leaned over the still-sitting Martha.

"Singing is one of my very favorite things to do," she said in an exact imitation of Martha's bell-like voice. "Why didn't you just get up and hug him?" she yelled at her friend, her only friend. "How could you make those cow eyes at him when you knew I was interested in him? How could you do that to me, Martha? How could you?"

# three

Martha's eyes opened wide. Then she got up. "I'm purely sorry, Rachel. I didn't know you were interested in Pastor Richards. And I didn't know I was making cow eyes at him." She stopped and giggled. "Truly, Rachel, I don't even know what cow eyes are, and besides I don't have the slightest interest in the man. Really, I don't."

Rachel felt chastened. If Martha had returned her anger she could have stayed mad. "Well," she muttered, "I'm not interested in him either. I just didn't want you making a fool of yourself."

Martha tinkled out another laugh. "Thanks, Rachel. I purely don't want to make a fool of myself."

A young girl approached them so they turned their attention to her. "Hello," she said hesitantly. "I'm Julia Tate. I bin watching you walking together havin' fun. I wondered if you'd mind if I walked with you sometime."

"We'd love to have you," Martha said instantly. "You just find us in the morning and join us."

Rachel didn't say anything but she wished Martha hadn't invited the kid. What made it worse, Martha sounded as if she had meant it. "How old are you?" Rachel asked.

"Sixteen," Julia replied. "How old are you?"

"I'm eighteen," Rachel said. "And Martha's seventeen. We've both finished high school." She hoped the girl would get the message that they were older. Then she remembered Thurman Tate. "You must be Thurman Tate's daughter," she said. "How are your oxen getting along with that horrendous load they have to pull?"

Julia looked perplexed. "All right, I guess. I don't pay

much attention to them. Were they sick or something?"

"No. Your father just refused the captain's orders to leave some heavy things in Independence."

Martha looked uncomfortable. "Well, you just come and walk with us tomorrow, Julia."

The girl left and Martha turned her attention back to Rachel. "We have to be kind to everyone," she said quietly. "Whatever we do for anyone, we're doing it for our Lord Jesus, you know."

Later that afternoon Rachel sat with her parents in their wagon, reading Scripture together, something she considered necessary but extremely boring.

"Hello," a young man's voice called from the outside. "Mr. Butler, could I talk to you a minute?"

Papa hopped to his feet, then down to the ground. Rachel sat quietly and listened.

"I just discovered we have an extra cow," the young man said, "and I don't know what to do with it."

A silence told Rachel that Papa didn't know either. All at once she remembered the man who'd been riding a cow. She jumped down beside her father. "I might know, Papa," she said. "Could we go see it?"

Sure enough, she recognized the cow as the one the man planned to ride to Oregon. "It belongs to the man who was going to Oregon on cowback," she said. "I saw him fall off her and try to catch her. I also saw him heading back to Independence on foot."

"Well," Nathan Butler said, "I guess it don't matter all that much, Ernie. Why don't you just leave her with ours for now."

The next morning, Martha and Rachel hadn't been walking an hour before Julia caught up with them. "What did you think of the preacher?" Rachel asked. "Handsome man, isn't he?"

Julia smiled shyly. "I guess. But he's too elegant for me. I like plain men better." She giggled. "But I like all men a lot."

A silly man-crazy girl! Rachel wondered how she'd put up with her all day every day. Maybe Julia would get tired and go back to her own wagon.

That afternoon a small dirty boy ran up to them from somewhere behind. "My name's Petey Piling," he said, puffing breathlessly. "Mama's sick and Papa told me to stay away so I won't bother them. Can I walk with you?"

Martha reached for his grimy hand. "Of course. You just walk right here between Willie and me. You two boys will have lots of fun together."

Ugh! Rachel bet Martha would welcome the most vile animal in the world. Why was she like that anyway? With the three big girls, the two little boys, and Josie, they had quite a group. Well, Rachel wasn't giving up her place to anyone.

The little boys started running around and yelling. Josie followed, yapping all the way. Martha acted as if she didn't hear a thing. "Can't you stop that racket?" Rachel asked.

Martha stopped talking and listened. Then she nodded. "They're all right," she said merrily. "We'll worry about them when someone starts crying."

Rachel felt like asking Martha if she planned to have any sanity left when they reached their destination, but she didn't. As she wished for some quiet, a small dirt clod hit her in the back. Spinning around she saw a look of surprise and fright on the two small faces.

"He didn't mean to hit you," Willie said. "Honest. Petey threw it at me and you just went and got in the way."

"It's all right," Martha said. "I'll brush her off. You all just go on and play." She moved to Rachel's side, brushed her off thoroughly, and finished with a few loving pats.

Only those pats kept Rachel's mouth shut and even then it wasn't easy. If she were in charge of those boys they'd be seen and not heard.

The next morning Rachel felt put out with the world in general and the extra people walking with them in particular. The boys had gotten cranky after a few miles but Martha didn't scold them. She started teaching them little songs. Afraid to say anything to Martha about the crowd she'd gathered around them, Rachel began on her favorite subject. "If God loved us even a little bit, we wouldn't be on this horrible journey."

"Not true, my friend," Martha said merrily. "God definitely wants us on this trip. There must be trappers or Indians we'll be telling about God's great love. For that matter there are people on this wagon train who don't know God. Like Mark Piling."

"If that's what we're going for I may start back right away," Rachel said. "I can think of a lot of boring things to do but that tops the list."

The boys and Julia walked with Martha and Rachel every day and no matter what they did Martha never became impatient.

One afternoon, Petey and Willie grew wilder than usual, tearing around and yelling at the top of their lungs; Josie was at their heels, adding her barking to the uproar. Just when Rachel thought she'd lose her sanity, Willie fell down. Petey fell over the top of him and into a mud puddle, thoroughly coating himself with the messy stuff.

"I can't walk in these clothes," the little boy wailed. He looked up into Martha's blue eyes. "Can I take them off, Martha? Can I?"

Martha winked at Rachel. "I'm not sure you should do that, Petey," she said. "But we'll take you to your wagon for fresh clothes. How will that be?"

Petey hung his head as though he'd rather just take off

the clothes. But he didn't say anything. Martha took his hand and also Willie's. "Come on, girls," she said to Rachel and Julia. "Let's find the Piling wagon."

Just about the time they found Petey's wagon the train stopped for the night. As they approached him, Mark Piling looked out of sorts. "Petey fell into a mud puddle," Martha said, laughing. "We brought him home for clean clothes."

Mr. Piling punched one of his oxen in the nose as he unyoked it; the ox grunted. Rachel stiffened and would have yelled at him if Martha hadn't poked her in the ribs. "I ain't got time to waste with you hoity-toity wimin," he snarled. "I'm too busy taking care of my sick wife. So go on back where you came from. How could I have clean clothes for anyone? What do you think I am, some kind of a nanny?" He turned toward the wagon. "Get down here and make a fire," he yelled into the wagon. "I'm hungry. I ain't laid in bed all day like you. Hurry up, woman!"

A moment later Sandy Piling's pale face appeared at the front of the wagon. She didn't speak to anyone but climbed down and looked around on the ground as though wondering what she could make a fire from.

"Want me to find you something to make a fire?" Martha asked.

"Get out of here before I take an whip to you!" Piling shouted, moving toward the girls. Petey, who'd been standing with Martha, flitted out of his father's way as if used to moving quickly. Rachel didn't need a second invitation. She took off like a deer, back to her own wagon.

"Wait for me," Julia yelled from somewhere behind but Rachel wasn't stopping for anyone. She put one foot in front of the other as fast as they'd go until she reached the Butler wagons where Mama squatted before a snapping campfire.

"What ever is after you, a bear?" Mama asked with a warm smile. Rachel waited until she caught her breath. "You said it just right, Mama," she finally got out. "Do you remember Mark Piling? He's the meanest man I've ever seen in my entire life. He really is. I hate him a whole lot."

"No you don't," Mama said. "You don't even know him. Tell me, what did he do to an animal?" She dumped some potatoes into bacon grease in a hot skillet. "This is the last of the potatoes until we find some to buy."

Just like Mama. She knew Rachel got upset when anyone abused an animal. But he did! "He did, Mama, but I got so mad at him later, I forgot all about it. He doubled up his fist and punched an ox in the face as hard as he could. But that's not all. He made his wife get out of the wagon to cook supper and she's real sick. Then he threatened to use a whip on us. You should have seen Petey get out of there. He's used to Mr. Piling hurting him, Mama."

Mama had stopped her meal preparations to listen to Rachel's wild story. "That's awful. What did you girls do to get him so riled up, love?" She picked up her bowl and started mixing the biscuits again.

"You know Petey walks with us all the time. Well, he fell into a puddle and wanted his clothes off really bad, so we took him to their wagon for clean clothes."

Mama had been shaping biscuits while Rachel talked. Now she put them into the dutch oven and laid it over the coals. "Sounds as if you didn't do a whole lot. The man's probably concerned about his wife. I've been hearing she's quite ill."

Strange way to show concern, Rachel thought. Well, she'd stay out of Mark Piling's way. Poor little Petey! He couldn't stay away all the time. But she could, and would.

"Would you take them some milk and cream?" Mama

asked as she poured some of each into bottles and capped them.

Rachel shook her head. "Mama! I just told you he threatened us with a whip. I'm not going over there for anything. Ever again."

"Can you stir the potatoes in a few minutes then?" Mama asked. Without waiting for an answer, she strode off toward the Piling wagon.

She returned a few minutes later, shaking her auburn head. "You're right, Rachel, he isn't very nice. But he accepted the milk and cream for his sick wife. Maybe it'll help her get well."

The next day, the train reached the Kansas River and camped at noon to prepare for the Sabbath.

Mama carried the tubs to the river and washed the family's clothes. She didn't ask Rachel to help and Rachel didn't offer. Down the river a ways, Martha worked over a scrub board; Rachel wandered over to talk to her. "How come you're doing your family's clothes?" she asked.

Martha looked up, her face red from exertion. "Oh, hello, Rachel," she said with a welcoming smile. "I'm doing the washing to help Mama. While I'm washing she's doing the baking for tomorrow. Haven't you heard that many hands make light work?"

Rachel thought about that as she wandered back to where Mama worked. When Mama looked up, her face was red from the hard work. Rachel felt a strong love tug at her heart. "Why don't you let me do that?" she asked. "You go back to camp and start the baking."

Mama looked relieved and, thanking Rachel, headed back to the wagons.

When Rachel finished an hour later, and had the clothes all hanging on the small bushes bordering the river, she ambled over to see why Martha wasn't finished yet.

"Well," Martha said. "I did finish our wash, but I'm doing the Pilings' right now."

Indignation turned Rachel's face red. "How could you be so dumb, Martha? Mr. Piling doesn't deserve to have one piece of his washing done for him."

Martha nodded, picked a little sock from the water, and scrubbed it on the board. "I know," Martha agreed. "But I'm not doing it for Mr. Piling. I'm doing it for Mrs. Piling and she purely needs all the help she can get."

On March twenty-seventh, the Sabbath, Pastor Richards preached and the women put another potluck meal together. Julia joined Martha and Rachel for the meal. When the girls had nearly finished their plates, two young men came and squatted near them in the grass. "Good afternoon," the tall skinny one said. "I'm Andy Shackleford. I hope you girls are enjoying the Sabbath rest."

"Oh, we surely are," Martha said. "And the good food. I believe I counted seven kinds of cake. God takes care of us even out here in the wild country. I'm Martha Lawford, and these are my friends, Julia Tate and Rachel Butler."

"And this is Ernie Cox. I believe he works for your father, Miss Butler."

"Oh." One of the oxen drivers, or herders. She didn't know, or care. She'd walk away from these yokels if it weren't for Martha. She couldn't do that to her special friend.

"Hello, Mr. Cox and Mr. Shackleford," Julia's young voice said. "We're glad to make yer acqu. . .acqui. . .we're glad to meet ya."

The two young men hardly gave Julia or Rachel a glance as they talked animatedly to Martha. Finally, they reluctantly left.

"I thought they'd never go," Rachel said. "I expected

any minute that you'd be inviting them to walk with us. You're way too friendly with people, you know."

Martha looked surprised. "I didn't know you could be too friendly with people, Rachel." She thought a moment and then broke into merry laughter. "Unless you make cow eyes at them."

That evening several people on the train heard strange sounds and knew for sure Indians were sneaking up on them. Captain Ransom called the people together and warned them. "Everyone better be watchin' every minute," he said. "Else you mayn't have another minute."

When Ransom finished, a young man moved in front of the people. "Hello," he said with a friendly smile. He stood over six-feet tall and looked lean but well muscled. His blondish hair hung over his ears but his closely trimmed darker beard and mustache looked dashing. "I'm Dan Barlow," he said. "I was just thinking what strange creatures we are. I wonder how many of you know that in 1825 the government took all the Indians' property and gave them Kansas for theirs. Now look what's happening," he said. "Here we are, invading their property by the thousands. I wonder what we'd do if thousands of people started taking our country from us?"

He stepped back into the crowd as quietly as he'd come.

Rachel sat up and took notice of Dan Barlow. That man makes sense, she told herself. I'm keeping my eye on him. Not too bad looking, either.

Another man stepped to the front. Middle-aged, the man looked kindly and round. "I'm George Rahn," he said. "I hope we all agree with our kind brother. I do. But I'm still afraid of the Indians so I suggest we watch carefully."

# four

Rachel fell asleep that night, frightened almost to death. She knew for sure she'd wake up with a tomahawk in her skull.

But the sun shone brightly the next morning and everything looked normal. Before they finished breakfast, George Rahn came around, laughing and joking. "I've been to nearly every wagon," he said, "and everyone seems to be all right and wearing his hair this morning."

That day Willie and Petey got into more trouble than usual. Willie's father had made him a little white horse from sticks and polished it up nice and smooth. Petey wanted the horse in the worst way and tried off and on all day to take it from Willie. Both boys ended up crying many times.

Rachel wished Martha would spank them both or at least give them a sound scolding. But Martha thought up some trail games. "Let's see what those white clouds look like," she said one time. "I see a sheep."

"I see a man with white hair," Willie said. "I think it's Jesus."

"I see a big white horse," Petey said just before lunging at Willie's horse again.

Finally, Martha stopped Petey and held him by the shoulders. "Petey, it's not nice to take things from other people," she said in her kind voice. "If you'll be really good the rest of the day I'll try to get Papa to make you a horse tonight."

A sun-laden smile covered Petey's face and he didn't

cause any more trouble.

That night one of the horse riders, Stan Latham, appeared at the Butler camp just before supper. Mama was baking biscuits and stirring bacon in a skillet. "You look beautiful tonight, ma'am," he said to Mrs. Butler. "And your culinary skills must approximate your beauty. The food smells totally aromatic."

Rachel felt like vomiting. But Papa only smiled and invited the man to eat with them. Mama kept the man's plate filled.

"Did you observe my herd of twenty-one of the east's finest horses?" he asked. "I'm planning to breed the best horses in the west and earn mountains of money. I'm sure horses will be badly needed there."

"I noticed your horses," Nate said. "Good looking bunch. Lots of luck."

During the meal Stan let slip a few words that Rachel wasn't accustomed to hearing.

After he left, Rachel scolded Papa for inviting such a dirty, sloppy, loud, and uncouth man to eat with them. "You wouldn't have let me associate with his kind in Quincy," she said. "Or were you fooled with his big words?"

Nate shook his head. "Not fooled, Rachel. But the man was hungry."

The next day, Willie held two smooth wooden horses. The moment Petey joined them, he held out the new one. Petey could hardly talk over his excitement. "I don't have any other toys," he said. "I like it." Martha had to keep after the boys who only wanted to get down on the ground and play with their horses. "Come on or we'll get left behind," she called. The boys would jump up, run a ways ahead of the girls, and flop onto the ground again for another few minutes of play.

That afternoon, clouds started gathering in the sky, hiding the sun. As the hours passed, it grew darker and more threatening. "Looks like rain," Martha said. Rachel hugged herself.

"I bet a thunderstorm's coming," Julia said. "I'm skeered of lightning and thunder."

"Thunder never hurt anyone," Rachel said. "Thunder tells you the lightning missed you."

About four o'clock, the first flash streaked across the sky to the west; thunder followed a little later. In a few minutes, the flashes grew brighter and the thunder followed, quicker and louder.

Josie crept along beside Martha, obviously frightened. The cattle began lowing and the horses grew nervous. Then the rain came. At first, infrequent big drops, then they grew smaller and came faster. Within ten minutes, a cold drenching rain poured over them.

"We'd better get into the wagons," Julia said, moving toward Rachel's.

"No," Martha said. "We won't melt any more than the animals will. We shouldn't make it harder on the oxen." Julia came back and the girls walked in the downpour. Josie, obviously delighted that the loud racket had stopped, ran and jumped and spun in the rain. Soon, the girls were soaked through and their feet were wet and muddy.

Then Rachel noticed the oxen struggling to pull the wagons. The wheels sank six inches into the mud. Several wagons stopped and drivers began yelling and then using their whips. The oxen pushed hard on their yokes but the wagons didn't move. The whips sang through the air then cracked on the animals' backs. The drivers' yells grew louder, the oxen's bawling made a terrible roar, but the wagons didn't move.

Suddenly, Rachel snapped. She ran to her own driver. "Stop abusing those animals!" she screamed into his face. "Can't you see they're trying their best? The wagons are stuck too hard." She stopped long enough to take in a few breaths of wet air. "You're supposed to be Christian on this wagon train so start acting like one or I'll grab that whip and use it on you!" She ran the length of the train, screaming the same words at every driver.

By the time she'd said it twenty times the drivers began to see she was right. No matter how hard the men whipped, no matter how loud the animals bawled, they simply couldn't pull the wagons through the mire. The men unloaded the wagons in the pouring rain. With water streaming down their faces, they put branches under the wagon wheels, and pried the wagon onto the branches until they came unmired. Then struggling, the oxen moved the empty wagons. Corralling the wagons, they made camp for the night.

The rain stopped as suddenly as it began. Rachel huddled away from the wagons and cried. She couldn't help it. How could anyone mistreat animals so horribly? Blood ran from the oxen's backs. She cried for the animals, then she cried for herself. Whatever on earth was she doing in this awful place? Heartbreak Trail. That's what it was.

Hearing more bawling, she looked back where Thurman Tate still whipped his oxen. Wait! She didn't see his things beside the trail. He hadn't unloaded! She ran right to him, grabbed the whip from his surprised hands, and dashed back to Captain Ransom. "That Tate man is still whipping his animals," she puffed, "and he didn't even unload."

Ransom nodded and headed toward Tate. Rachel threw the whip as hard as she could, about eight feet, and followed the captain. "I thought we all understood we had to unload," Ransom said quietly to Tate.

Tate replied with an oath. "Ain't no one'd help me," he finally got around to saying. "I can't do it alone so them oxen'll just have to work harder." He looked at Rachel, standing a ways back. "You better get that there wild woman under control if you know what's good for her."

"I'll find someone to help you," the captain said, hurrying away. "Come on, Miss Butler," he said when he passed Rachel. "You'd better stay away from that man."

Rachel helped Mama make a fire with wet wood, then cook supper on a sizzling smoky fire. As they ate, she noticed about ten men approach Tate, unload a heavy cookstove from his wagon, a large chiffonier, and other things. Then the oxen managed to pull the wagon from the mud and into the circle.

After the Butler family finished eating, Rachel stood by the fire, drying her clothes. She and her parents dried their featherbeds and quilts, holding them before the fire, turning them every few minutes.

A young man approached the fire, one of the men who had helped Tate unload his heavy stuff. Rachel noticed several patches on his clothes and holes that needed mending. He wasn't all that clean either. "Hello," he said to Rachel. "I just wanted to tell you I'm elated to find someone brave enough to stand up for the helpless animals. I wish I'd done it, but I didn't and you did. Even a big oxen is helpless when a man starts on him and I agree it's time we considered their feelings, too. Thanks again, Miss Butler." He walked off into the night.

Rachel thought about him after she climbed into her featherbed. The man was a mess, but he cared about animals. She'd thought maybe she was the only one in the whole world who did.

The next morning the sun shone brightly and the people dried their belongings before they started. The same young men who'd unloaded Tate's wagon reloaded it. Rachel heard some of them asking Tate if he wouldn't like to leave the cookstove there to save his oxen. "Never!" he said. "Them oxen are just lazy. After getting away with what they did yesterday they'll be worse now."

The next morning Rachel grumbled to Martha about Tate and what an awful man he was. "I hate that man," Rachel said. "I really hate him. I hate Heartbreak Trail, too."

"It's hard all right," Martha said. Then she giggled. "I was purely surprised to hear you yelling at all those men. But the men may be kinder to their animals now."

"I feel just like you, Rachel," Julia said. "Those oxen feel pain just like we do and it's cruel to whip them when they can't work any harder."

For the first time ever, Rachel felt kindly toward Julia. When she thought about Julia's father, she could hardly talk to Julia. Now she knew Julia wasn't just a young copy of Tate. Come to think of it, she'd noticed that the girl's parents never checked on her or seemed to care where she was. Hmmm. Julia and Petey were somewhat alike. No one cared about either of them. She really did have something for which to be thankful. Both her mama and papa loved her dearly and would do anything in the world for her.

April third was the Sabbath and Pastor Richards led the group in singing again and preached a fitting sermon. Then, he acted as if Martha were of utmost importance to him and Rachel hated every minute of it.

The next day they'd traveled a few hours when one of the horse riders reported a large band of Indians ahead.

Captain Ransom stopped the train, calling a meeting of the men to decide if they should corral the wagons or keep going. They decided to keep going with weapons loaded and ready.

When they reached the Indians riding spotted ponies, they discovered they wore complete war outfits, including feathers, and held large bows in their hands. Rachel, her heart racing, the saliva dry in her mouth, marched with Martha, their heads high. The stench of the Indians, combined with her terror, made Rachel physically ill. It seemed as if those columns of Indians and ponies would never end but the savages looked dead ahead, never glancing in the direction of the wagon train. Someone counted 1,500 Indians.

After they passed, Rachel felt such a relief that she got silly; so did Martha and Julia. They laughed at everything and nothing. "What's funny?" Petey kept asking but the girls just laughed some more.

Day after day they traveled on. Rachel appreciated and loved Martha more every day. She still wished Julia and Petey and even Willie didn't have to be there all the time, but she grew somewhat used to them. After all, where else could they be?

Julia kept talking about a man she'd seen. "He's tall and blond," she said. "You have to see him."

"Show him to us next time you see him," Rachel said.

One afternoon, Martha acted strange, and Rachel wondered what had happened. Maybe she'd seen a man, too. The preacher acted as if Martha were the only girl on the train but she didn't seem to return the feeling. Maybe she'd seen someone else. Finally, Martha told her. "I'm purely embarrassed to tell you, but my brother Jackson shot a rabbit this morning and Mama asked me to dress it. I've never done such a thing, but I'm going to do it if it kills me."

"Why would you be embarrassed?" Rachel asked. "I've never even touched a dead animal, let alone fix it to eat."

Martha heaved a relieved sigh. "Maybe you'd like to watch me fix it," she offered as if she could use the moral support.

That evening Rachel watched but didn't help. She couldn't figure out how such a horrible looking mess could turn into something so delicious.

The next evening, as the men corralled the wagons and unyoked the oxen, Tate's animals didn't move fast enough to suit him so his whip whistled as he used it on their backs. The animals bawled as Tate yelled and whipped hide from their backs. Some nearby oxen stampeded, running over several men and into the circled wagons. When they got everything under control, they found Andy Shackleford, Dan Barlow, and another man hurt and two oxen badly cut up.

The young man who'd thanked Rachel for standing up for the oxen came with a black bag. First he checked the men and told them they had no broken bones but were badly bruised and to take it easy for a few days. Then he got some stuff out of his bag and began sewing up the oxen. Several men held the animals but the young man doing the sewing kept talking kindly to them. They seemed to understand and stood still. Rachel had never seen anyone so quietly kind to both men and animals. Different from most of the people around for sure. Come to think about it, she hadn't heard him spit out any filthy words either.

The next morning she asked Martha about the man.

"Don't you know who that was?" Martha asked. "He's Dr. Thomas Dorland, a brand new doctor. I heard someone say he's planning to make a difference in the lives of the pioneers. He's one of the horse riders."

"You mean he doesn't have a wagon?"

Martha giggled. "No wagon. Everything he has, including his medical supplies, is in that bag behind his saddle."

Rachel shook her head. "I don't understand how he can live like that." Then she thought of herself and giggled. "But I don't understand how I'm living like this either."

At dusk that evening a small group of Indians approached the wagon train. The men loaded their guns and stood watch. Rachel didn't have a gun but she watched the approaching group too, counting five ponies and five men. But when they neared the train, one looked like a woman.

A white woman at that, bareheaded with faded brown hair. When they reached the first wagon, ten men surrounded the Indians, their guns pointed at the ground. The woman jumped from her pony to the ground. "Don't look so scared," she said loudly. "We're friends." She took her pony's reins and handed them to the closest Indian. The Indians turned the ponies and headed back the way they'd come.

The woman, as big as most men, grinned. "Well? You got room for one more?"

"What's going on?" Captain Ransom asked quietly.

"Hello," the woman stuck out a hand, "I'm Deborah Petty, genuine white woman, nothing to fear."

Ransom shook her hand.

"I went mushroom picking yesterday and somehow got lost. Before I found my train, three white snakes got me. They weren't about to help me back to my train so I started screaming my head off." She laughed loudly. "Imagine how I felt when four redskins charged up. I figured we'd all lose our scalps and thought it might be worth losing mine just to see those white savages lose theirs."

"I see you're still wearing your hair," George Rahn said with a grin.

The woman laughed. "Yes and so are my captors. The Indians scared them plenty but didn't harm them. Anyway, when they saw this wagon train they brought me here and that's the story. They fed me and kept me last night, so my opinion of what color savages are has changed a bit."

Mrs. Ransom put her arms around the big woman and held her close. "You can share our wagon, Deborah. We'll work it out. But what about your train? Do you have a husband on it?"

"Naw. I'm all alone in the world. If you got room for me, one train's as good as the next." She laughed nervously. "You can see I'm plenty big. I like to work so I can earn my room and board."

As the days wore on, it seemed to Rachel that the mornings were getting colder rather than warmer. She kept putting on more clothes every morning and still froze. "I'm going to have to help more with the cooking," she told Mama, "so I can hang around the fire." She'd been helping some lately and found she didn't mind at all.

The train came to Big Blue River and found no bridge or ferry. The river wasn't wide but was about three feet deep. The men led the oxen in pulling the wagons cross and the women rode horseback. Rachel hung back almost to the last. Already freezing, she wasn't eager to get wet. Finally, Papa told her she had to go. He and Mama rode their geldings and Rachel her mare. "Tuck your dress up as the water comes up," Papa said, "and you won't get wet."

"Somebody might see me," Rachel wailed.

Papa shrugged. "Do as you please."

Lifting her dress modestly over her knees, Rachel gritted her teeth as Ginger, her horse, stepped into the water. She leaned forward and patted the horse's sleek neck. "It'll be cold for you too, baby," she said softly. But the horse didn't seem to mind the water. After a bit Rachel decided the water would come only a little above her knees so she tried to get used to the cold. When they passed the middle, Rachel heaved a sigh. Papa said everything looks harder than it is and this hadn't been all that bad.

Just at that moment, Ginger dropped from under Rachel.

With no time to prepare, Rachel found herself in the cold water, gasping as she took in a big swallow. Burdened with all her clothes, she couldn't seem to get herself above the water.

Briefly, she heard men and women yelling, then forgot all about anyone else as she tried to swim. But she couldn't catch her breath, she just couldn't.

# five

The next thing Rachel knew was that she felt herself choking and that she still couldn't pull in any breath. Opening her eyes, she found herself lying on her stomach on some grass. Then something pressed on her back and water poured into her mouth from her throat. She choked some more.

"Cough hard," a soft male voice said. "Try hard, Miss Butler. Just keep trying to breathe. You're all right now."

She didn't know who spoke and felt too tired to look. Then the pressure started on her back again and some more water came into her mouth. After a little while she could breathe though it hurt and made a raspy sound.

Then someone turned her over. She looked into the soft eyes of Dr. Dorland. He smiled at her. "You gave us a scare, but you just need to breathe and cough a while now."

Suddenly, Papa dropped to his knees beside her, gathering her to him. "My lassie," he said brokenly, "we'd have lost you if this young man hadn't pulled you out."

Young man? Rachel looked around but saw only Dr. Dorland.

"Yes," Papa said. "Dr. Dorland swam out and pulled you to safety."

"What happened?" Rachel rasped.

"Ginger stepped into a hole and went under. But you're both all right."

Dr. Dorland, who'd been on his knees beside Rachel, got to his feet. "I might as well go find my horse now if you don't need me anymore. Don't hesitate to call me if you feel anxious about anything."

Rachel tried to sit up. Papa helped her. Mama knelt down beside her and hugged her. "I love you, child," she said.

Rachel soon walked to the wagon that had been corralled with the others. She didn't feel too terrible except she still coughed some. Mama made some bean soup that went down easily. Rachel began to feel stronger.

During the night of April ninth, a cold wind arose and Rachel felt chilled right into her bones. She didn't get up for breakfast but Mama brought her some hot oatmeal with cream. It tasted better than almost anything Rachel had ever eaten in her life.

The fierce north wind forced Pastor Richards to cancel the Sabbath's preaching service and potluck dinner. People huddled in their wagons or around their fires, trying to keep warm. Papa read some Bible chapters to Mama and Rachel then said they'd pray together.

"I'm not praying," Rachel said. "If the Lord loved us even a tiny bit we wouldn't be out here in the middle of nowhere."

"That's enough, Rachel," Papa said sternly. "God didn't force you to come on the Trail. I did. You can be mad at me or yell at me or refuse to talk to me. But you're to stop blaspheming God at once. Do you understand?"

Rachel nodded, almost ashamed of her outburst. Almost.

The following week, the train crossed the Big Sandy River then the Little Sandy and followed it for several days. The weather improved; Rachel's spirits lifted, too.

One day she noticed the oxen's necks were bleeding from the pressure of the yokes. Rachel felt so sorry for the animals she went off by herself and cried again. Why did the animals suffer so for men's stupidity? Rachel wouldn't consider making the oxen pull her weight in the wagon now. Besides, she enjoyed walking with Martha. Sometimes though, she wished Martha weren't so perfect. Then she realized that that's why she loved her friend and why everyone else did, too.

One day, Willie and Petey seemed extra cranky. Every afternoon the boys took a nap in the Lawford wagon but it wasn't nooning time yet. Rachel wished it were.

Martha never lost patience with the two little boys. Never. This day she got them into a game thanking God for blessings. The boys, each trying to think of more blessings than the other, forgot to fuss. When they finally grew tired of this game, Julia got them started naming the animals God has waiting for them in heaven. The boys liked that game almost as well as Martha's and searched their minds for animals until nooning time.

The train reached the Little Blue River and traveled along it for several days. Rachel helped Mama with the cooking and cleaning up now. The green willow sticks, their only fuel, put out a pungent smoke that always got into Rachel's eyes. "Smoke follows beauty, you know," Papa said, winking at his only child. "It couldn't find anyone prettier than my two lassies."

"So how do you explain the bugs?" Rachel asked. "They get into everything, even the food we're cooking."

Mama smiled and stirred the biscuit mix. "One thing the Trail's teaching us is not to be so picky. We just have to take the bugs out of the food before we eat it."

Rachel knew that. But she hated it.

They camped early on Saturday to prepare for the Sabbath. Rachel and Martha did their families' washings then Martha washed Mrs. Piling's things. The poor woman didn't seem to be getting any better.

Mama and Rachel made several kinds of cakes with their supply of milk and cream. The cows' milk supply had dwindled but they still gave enough to share with several families.

With the warmer calmer weather they would have preaching and a potluck dinner. They made do without eggs and no one seemed to notice. They also fixed a big pot of baked beans in the dutch oven for the meal.

Rachel hated to admit it even to herself but she looked forward to the next day, especially for the chance to see Pastor Richards.

That evening, several men came to see Papa, telling him they'd dallied enough on the Sabbath and that they should all get together and tell Captain Ransom they wanted to get going.

"I wouldn't think of it," Papa said. "The oxen have sore necks, sore feet, and they're losing weight. They need the day to catch up. Trust the good Lord to know what's best, brothers."

The next morning, about the time the preaching began, Rachel saw some women carrying tubs to the river. What were they doing? Not washing on the Sabbath! Then they heard the men pounding on the wagons and saw two of them heading out with their guns.

Rachel, who couldn't care less about the Sabbath, felt shock ripple through her body. No one ever worked on the Sabbath! After sitting in shock for a while, not hearing a word Pastor Richards said, she began giggling to herself. What was she expecting? The Lord to send fire from heaven to consume the Sabbath breakers?

She turned her attention back to the preaching. The reverend was telling the people that Christ's children find ways to serve Him, even in the wilderness. The working field is still there, only smaller. She wondered if she could help Martha a little more with the children. Julia did. If they both helped, it would unburden Martha a lot.

After dinner Rachel went to the minister. "Would helping take care of children be the kind of ministering you meant?" she asked.

His smile was sincere. "It certainly would. And it would help you as much as the children's mother." Someone else crowded in to ask the man a question so Rachel went back to her seat. A lot of good that did. She got to talk to him for about two minutes.

A little later the pastor found Martha, and Rachel watched them talking and laughing together for some time. A lot more than two minutes!

"Ah, there you are," Jackson Lawford said, squatting beside Rachel. "Where you been hiding out? Did you make any of the grub I ate?"

"I'm afraid I wouldn't know," Rachel said in a cold voice. "I have better things to do than watch whose food you eat."

Jackson didn't hang around long, exactly what Rachel wanted. She wanted to be alone in case the Reverend wanted to come talk to her. But he didn't. At one point she caught Dr. Dorland watching her but when their eyes met, he turned away.

The next day they left the Little Blue River to enter the Platte River Valley, so level you could see seven miles. "Look," Petey said, "the grass is getting greener every day."

"Yes," Martha told him with a smile. "I'll bet the oxen like that, don't you?"

"Can we pick some and take it to them?" Willie asked.

"Not now," Rachel said. "The oxen are working. Why

don't you wait until almost nooning time, then pick a big bunch for them? I'll help you."

One day Jackson told Martha they were seeing antelopes but couldn't get close enough to shoot.

"Good," Rachel said. "They're too beautiful to shoot."

"You don't mean that," Jackson said. "We're all in desperate need of meat."

Rachel thought that over. Almost all the meat they'd had on the trail was dried side meat. But she still didn't want them to kill the antelope.

The next day three men rode to meet the train. When they reached the wagons, they asked Captain Ransom if the people needed meat. When assured they did, the men gave them four skinned and gutted antelopes.

"How do you happen to have all this extra meat?" Rachel heard Ransom ask the men.

"We found the herd and knew someone would need meat," they answered. "Meat's been scarce lately so we just got it while we could."

"Much obliged," Nate said. "Where you fellows headed?"

"Salt Lake City," one of the men replied.

Pastor Richards seemed to come alive at the name of the town. "You must be Mormons," he said softly.

"That we are," the last man said. "And we'd best be on our way. You folks enjoy the meat."

"I have your trail guidebook," Nate said. "In fact, most of us have a copy. I don't know how we'd have gotten along without it."

One of the men pulled a battered copy from a deep pocket. "We use it, too," he said with a pleased smile. The men saluted, turned their horses, and took off down the trail ahead of the Ransom Train.

As the train lumbered along, some stopped wagons

appeared on the Trail in front of them.

"They must be having trouble," Martha said. "I hope it isn't sickness."

But when they reached the wagons it seemed the train was having internal strife.

"Can we help you folks?" Captain Ransom asked one of the sullen looking men.

The men, having a severe disagreement, didn't even hear Ransom speaking.

Rachel, Martha, Julia, and the boys moved close enough to listen.

The men argued whether to continue or go back. "We're already out of food," someone said, "and we're not half-way yet. If we continue, we're sure to starve."

"That's your problem," a loud voice answered. "You knew it was a long way when we left. Let's go on," he said to the others gathered around. The people seemed about evenly divided in their desire to return to Independence or continue on.

After bickering another fifteen minutes, one of those who wanted to continue on turned to Ransom. "Maybe those with guts enough to go on can join your train," he said to the captain.

"You can join us if you're Christian and if you can keep up," Ransom said.

"We'll make them oxen keep up," the man said. Ransom extended his hand. The other man grasped it and they shook.

Hearing the conversation, Rachel didn't like the men. They didn't care a thing about their animals and wouldn't hesitate to mistreat them. She wished they hadn't joined the train. But they didn't treat their animals any differently than their own people treated theirs.

One day she noticed again their own oxen's raw and

bleeding necks. The animals' tongues hung from their mouths as if they didn't have strength to hold them up. Many of the animals limped badly. Rachel's heart felt as if it would break as the drivers forced them on. She ran and threw her arms around one of the bleeding necks. "I'm so sorry," she whispered, tears running dusty trails down her cheeks.

"Get out of there!" the driver yelled. "You're in the way."

Rachel dropped her arms and turned to the driver. "You don't even care about these animals!" she screamed. "I hate every one of you. You're worse than animals. Why should the animals have to suffer so much for man's stupidity?" A moment later she covered her face with her arms and moved back beside Martha.

Martha stopped walking and crushed Rachel in a big hug. "I'm sorry for them too," she whispered into Rachel's ear. "But no one knows what to do. Whether we go on or go back to Independence, we can't do it without the oxen." She pushed Rachel back so they could see each other. Tears ran in muddy streams down her face, too. "What can we do?" she whispered.

Rachel shook her head. She didn't know, but she couldn't bear what they were doing. The rest of the day all five walkers remained quiet.

On Sunday, April twenty-fourth, Rachel once again awakened to men's rough voices at dawn. Why couldn't people catch on that this was a rest day? The only day they got to sleep late. She turned over and pulled the pillow over her head. She still heard the commotion so she jumped out of her featherbed, dressed, and then dropped over the side of her wagon.

The new men had Captain Ransom surrounded. "We

didn't bargain for setting around all day," one of them said. "We gotta get going or we'll be caught in the mountains in the winter."

"I told you this is a Christian train," Ransom replied calmly. "We figure we and our animals need the rest." He motioned west with his thumb. "If you don't agree, nobody's holding you here. Just meander on down the trail."

"You tryin' to get rid of us?" one of the men bellowed.

"Nope," Ransom said. "Ain't tryin' to hold you here, neither."

"Who crowned you king and lord of everythin'?" one yelled.

Two others came at Ransom with their fists flying. Ransom barely had time to look surprised before receiving several hard blows to his face that put him on the ground, dazed.

# six

Daniel Barlow, evidently hearing the fracas, came roaring into the midst of the trouble, punching both men's faces with hard staccato strikes. The two turned on Barlow who could nearly handle both. As the men pounded each other, Captain Ransom struggled to his feet. "Stop it!" he shouted, "or you'll all leave this train immediately." The fists continued flying, most ending with a low thud and groans.

Ransom thrust himself into the middle of the brawl still yelling at the top of his voice for them to stop. For some reason they all stopped and stood staring at the brave man.

Someone called Dr. Dorland who arrived soon with his little black satchel. On examining the men he found all three cut up enough to need stitches. Rachel moved up almost beside him as he cleaned the wounds and gently stitched them up, all the while talking quietly to the men. Not a word of recrimination, just fixing them the best he could. He was a real doctor, worthy of the title.

Dan Barlow thanked Dr. Dorland several times for his help; the other men said nothing. After the doctor finished, they yoked up their oxen, packed their wagons, and left the train.

The camp seemed exceptionally quiet as the remaining people built fires and prepared breakfasts.

"Wasn't Dr. Dorland wonderful?" Rachel asked her parents. "I've never seen anyone so quiet yet so kind. He's very dedicated."

Mama and Papa agreed then they all hurried to the

preaching service.

Pastor Richards spoke about doing to others as we would have them do to us. "If everyone lived that way," he said, "there would be no more trouble between people—ever. Afterwards, Rachel made it a point to tell him she appreciated his talk and how much she agreed with him. "Thank you," he said with an appreciative smile. "You have no idea how much it helps a pastor to know how his congregation feels about his sermons." By that time several people crowded around, distracting him with their silly comments. Rachel stomped off feeling rejected. She hurried home to help Mama with the food for the potluck dinner.

As usual, Martha, Julia, and Rachel ate on a quilt on their own little spot of ground. They'd barely sat down when Julia started going on about Dan Barlow.

"Wasn't that brave of him to protect Captain Ransom?" she asked. "He'd have beat them both up if the captain hadn't stopped him."

Rachel laughed at the younger girl. "I thought it was pretty dumb," she said. "One against two is never good."

Just then Dan stopped beside them. "Did I hear my name used in vain?"

"I hope not," Rachel said. "I just said two against one is bad."

"I think you were brave," Julia said. "Do you feel all right now?"

"Mind if I sit down?" he asked, settling on the ground near them. "I feel fine. That's one good doc we have. I say we're a lucky train."

"I do, too," Martha said. "We've needed a doctor several times and who knows how many more times we may yet?"

Soon Pastor Richards joined them, seating himself

beside Dan. He seemed to direct most of his comments toward Martha.

"You have quite a varied congregation," Rachel said. "Have you found out if everyone is really Christian?"

"I'm not a judge," he said. "If people say they're Christians, they are." He continued his discussion with Martha about caring for two little boys on the Trail.

As the little group talked, Rachel felt someone looking at her and raised her eyes to a group of men standing nearby. Sure enough, she met Dr. Dorland's soft gray eyes. He turned away so quickly his sun-streaked hair flipped across his face. What a kind, gentle face. But why was he watching her?

The next day, the wagon train reached Fort Kearney. Rachel had been looking forward to this because she expected a glimpse of civilization. But it wasn't to be. The frame houses of the four officers looked passable but the rest were made of sunburnedbrick. The fort, fences, and outbuildings were made from dirt cut into blocks and stacked up. They called it adobe. Fort Kearney was set up by the government to guard the Oregon Trail. Papa's Mormon guidebook said the fort was 319 miles from Independence, too far to turn back.

Fort Kearney disappointed Rachel a lot and the officers looked more like fur trappers than government men.

After passing the fort, the train reached the Platte River and followed it. Several men in rough boats tried to navigate the wide but shallow river.

"What are you doing?" Julia called as they walked past.

"Trying to catch some fish," one young man said. "We run aground fifty times each day and spend half our time on sand bars." He grinned as if he didn't mind as much as he might.

As they walked along the river, other men called to the girls and Julia always answered. "Don't you know young ladies don't talk to strange men?" Rachel scolded.

Martha laughed. "I don't think it hurts anything, Rachel. There's enough of us here to protect her. It's kind of fun to hear what they're doing, don't you think?"

A strange unearthly racket interrupted and the girls looked down the Trail toward the sound. A huge line of Indians pressed toward them, some walking, some on ponies. The Indians screamed, howled, and made war whoops that nearly broke Rachel's ear drums. Suddenly, she felt ready to run back home, on foot, all by herself.

But as they neared the Indians, she saw several men carrying a body on their shoulders. The dead man wore a complete headdress and war paint, making it look pathetically fierce. The girls laughed hysterically with relief knowing the Indians didn't mean them any harm. Besides that, the Indians were making so much noise they'd never hear the girls' talking and laughing. Finally, the Indians passed.

"I wonder if that poor man knew our Saviour," Martha wondered out loud.

Julia and Rachel burst into laughter again. "Tell me, how could he?" Rachel asked.

Martha nodded. "Probably not. That's why we're here, Rachel, to share our wonderful God with them and everyone else."

"Spare me," Rachel said. "I'm not sharing anything with anyone." But inwardly she admired Martha and envied her unwavering faith.

The next day they came to the south fork of the Platte River where they had to cross. The river was half a mile wide but very shallow. "The problem," the men explained, "is the quicksand in spots."

Making sure the animals had all they wanted to drink so they wouldn't stop during the ford, the men hooked several wagons together with eight to ten yoke of oxen for each wagon. The oxen drivers worked with their own animals while other men swam and waded, digging out the wagons as necessary.

The girls and little boys stood on the bank and watched. Andy Shackleford, Dan Barlow, Tom Dorland, Stan Latham, and Ernie Cox worked in the water.

"Who's that big fellow beside Andy?" Julia asked.

Rachel and Martha burst into laughter. "That's not a fellow," Rachel said. "That's Debbie Petty, the woman the Indians brought to the train."

"Well, she's working like a man," Julia said. "I wish I could help."

"Go ahead," Rachel said.

"No, you don't," Martha said. "Debbie's bigger and stronger than most women. You'll just be satisfied to watch. Understand?"

As they watched, the string of wagons stopped and the men flew into action, pushing, lifting, shoving, and shouting. Using a shovel, Debbie frantically pawed mud from around the sinking wagon wheels. At the same time the drivers urged the oxen to pull even harder. When the wagons began moving again, the watching people cheered loudly.

Finally, the last wagon emerged from the water and Captain Ransom called corralling.

As Rachel helped Mama fix supper, she wished Pastor Richards would come calling. He was so good looking, educated, and always clean. Come to think of it, she never saw him except on Sabbaths. She wondered where he kept himself and what he did during the week.

That night Rachel awakened in the night feeling

something on her face. She brushed her hand across it and felt bugs. Lots of bugs! Jumping from her bed in the dark she brushed over her face, arms, chest, and back. They seemed to be everywhere. She tried to sweep her bed clean with her hand but, being in the dark, she felt unsure.

After blindly cleaning herself and her bed several times, she gingerly climbed back under the covers and fell asleep almost at once. Some time later, she awakened again with bugs marching across her face. Jumping up, she went through the wild sweeping off of the bugs from the bed and herself and fell asleep again, exhausted.

Several more times the bugs, walking across her face, awakened her. Each time she fell asleep more exhausted than the last time. Finally, dawn broke and the train began to awaken.

That day everyone laughed and joked about the dor-bugs as they called them. Rachel didn't say a word but she found nothing funny about the insects, even though assured they don't bite.

"They come out of a hole in the ground," Julia said. "My dad told me they won't hurt you. They just run across your face fifty times. He says we'll get used to them and sleep right through."

Not me, Rachel thought. Never!

At least the dor-bugs came out only at night. Many other kinds of bugs swarmed over them during the whole day from dawn to dusk. Sometimes they bit, sometimes they didn't, but red welts covered most everyone's body, especially the children's bodies.

Just before serving the beans, Mama scooped the bugs from them. Even so, Rachel always had to spoon out many bugs while she ate. As she did, she remembered how she hated the Trail. Most of the time she didn't think about it anymore. Just sometimes.

At Plum Creek the horse riders spotted a single buffalo ahead, the first one they'd seen. Some of the men rode out after it and two hours later they returned, many of them with parts of the buffalo hanging over their horses.

That evening they had another of their rare celebrations with music and dancing. The people ate all the meat they could hold. The next day they jerked the rest of the meat before moving on.

As they traveled, the sand began deepening until it became hard to walk on. The oxen strained pulling the wagons, even on flat ground. Wildflowers, starting to bloom on the prairie, sent out a fragrance that brightened the day.

One day they met a wagon with four rough-looking men walking beside it. "We've been up and down this trail," they said. "It gets lots worse. The oxen won't be able to pull the wagons. You won't even be able to walk in the deep hot sand. Your oxen will all die on this trail and most of you will, too."

"Don't put too much stock in what those men said," Captain Ransom told them after the men left. "Something made them bitter."

Nevertheless, the girls, Rachel, Julia, and Martha trembled, remembering what the men had said. The little boys didn't play or fuss as usual either.

That night they camped on the north fork of the Platte River, two miles short of Ash Hollow, 504 miles from Independence, the guidebook said.

Martha and Rachel discovered an empty little cabin near the Trail. Inside they found hundreds of letters addressed to nearly everywhere in the world.

"Why would people leave them here?" Martha asked.

Rachel shook her head. "I don't know. Maybe they

thought someone would see their letter and would take it to the address on the envelope." As they looked through the envelopes, a noise outside caused them to drop to the floor.

"Shh," Rachel said. "Maybe they won't see us."

When the door creaked open and two men walked in, Rachel thought her heart would beat through her chest. But when the men's voices reached her ears, she recognized them! Andy Shackleford and Dan Barlow.

About that time Martha laughed and scrambled to her feet. "You nearly scared the daylights out of us," she said to the men.

Rachel crawled from her hiding place. "You caught us," she said. "What are you going to do with us?"

Andy laughed. "Do you know it's getting dark? We're going to see you safely back to your wagons. How's that?"

The next morning Rachel didn't waste any time telling Julia that Martha and she spent some time in a log cabin with Andy and Dan.

"How come you didn't take me?" Julia cried. "You knew I'd want to go."

"Because we didn't know we'd see them," Martha said sweetly. "We just found the cabin at the same time they did. We didn't even spend time with them. We went right back to our wagons. That's all there was to it."

That day the sand and dust grew deeper, spilling over Rachel's high-top shoes. The dust rose until it caused her eyes to burn and water; soon, they were sore and inflamed. Willie and Petey became cross and fretful. Martha, unmindful of her own discomfort, soothed the little ones the best she could.

Rachel noticed the oxen stumbling blindly along, their eyes nearly closed against the blowing dust. She ran and dipped her handkerchief into the river and tried to clean one of her ox's eyes. The ox tried to jerk its head away from her hand.

"Get out of there!" the driver yelled at her. "You tryin' to get hurt? Or just gettin' in the way?"

Rachel withdrew, knowing by now it didn't help to argue with the drivers.

The train camped early due to the dust. After Martha and Rachel finished their washings and other work, they explored and found many different kinds of flowers, including wild orchids, dainty pinkish flowers hiding in the shade of larger bushes, broken branches, or whatever.

Several kinds of butterflies flitted among the flowers—huge yellow-and-black ones, small brightly colored ones, and everything in between. As she watched the beautiful creatures fluttering through the air, Tom Dorland appeared from somewhere.

# seven

"Kind of pretty, aren't they?" Tom asked quietly.

"Yes," Rachel whispered. "I love them."

Stepping a few feet away, he broke a twig and carried it to Rachel. "Here's one that's fresh out of its chrysalis. Let's watch it." He carefully transferred the yellow-and-black creature with crumpled wings to Rachel's finger where it clung. "It's a tiger swallowtail," he said. "And no, it isn't crippled. That's the way they look at first."

They didn't talk anymore as they watched it beat its wings up and down, up and down. Gradually, the wings grew fuller and less crumpled. Then, the little hooks at the bottoms of its huge wings straightened and took on many colors—pinks, blues, lavenders.

"It's beautiful," she whispered softly, holding her hand perfectly still.

"Shhhh," he whispered. "It's about ready to fly."

As they watched, it lifted its big wings one more time and fluttered into the sky. Rachel didn't want the experience to end.

She turned to the doctor. "Thank you, Dr. Dorland. That was the most beautiful thing I've ever seen in my entire life. And I'd have never seen it if you hadn't happened to be here."

"I enjoyed it, too," he said, turning away. "Thanks for sharing the moment."

After he left, Rachel lost interest in continuing her investigation. On her way back to her wagon, she brushed several metallic-looking green beetles from her clothes.

As dusk neared, sand flies and mosquitoes swarmed from the river, biting her face and hands.

On Sunday, May first, the morning wind and dust died down in the afternoon so Pastor Richards invited everyone to a hymn sing and preaching service. Rachel enjoyed watching the man who always looked as if he lived in Independence rather than on Heartbreak Trail. She didn't necessarily admit it even to herself but she enjoyed the songs, too. A few people played instruments and everyone else sang with whole hearts. Although Papa had asked several times, Rachel left her guitar in the wagon.

Pastor Richards told the people in his sermon that faith is the most important thing for a Christian. "We must spend time in the Word," he said, "and pray until our faith grows so strong it cannot fail."

Afterward, Rachel told him she agreed with him that faith was an all-important necessity to a Christian. "I work on my faith all the time," she gushed.

He gave her a brilliant smile. "Please, don't work on it," he advised. "Just spend a lot of time reading His Word and communicating with Him in prayer." As usual, people crowded between them.

Later, the people all brought their suppers together for a potluck meal. Pastor Richards joined the girls, sitting near them on the bare ground.

"I'm so glad you joined us," Rachel said eagerly. "I've been wanting to discuss a theological problem with you." She searched frantically for something she could bring up that would interest the young minister.

He held up a big hand. "No deep talks today," he said smiling to soften his words. "I'm here to relax." Then, he turned to Martha. "Still planning to walk all the way to Oregon?"

She laughed. "We all are, Rachel, Julia, and me. Even the little boys walk all the time except for when they nap."

Pastor Richards laughed with her. "How are the shoes holding up?"

Dan Barlow appeared and sat down beside Pastor Richards. "This looks like the most interesting conversation around. Mind if I join you?"

Jackson Lawford folded his long frame down beside the other men. "Needing a little protection, sis?"

Rachel sighed heavily. With so many people, Pastor Richards would never notice her. She got to her feet, her empty plate still in her hand. "If you'll excuse me, I should go check on my folks. Nice to see you all."

One more wasted Sabbath, she thought as she ambled toward her wagon. Well, maybe *Pastor Richards* would see now that she wasn't chasing him. As she thought about it she wondered if he hadn't given his best smiles to Julia today.

The next morning Rachel had nearly finished breakfast when she heard Martha screaming, "Help, someone help, quick!"

Rachel ran back to the Lawford wagon about the time a dozen other people reached the site of Martha's cries. Martha stood beside Josie, who lay on the ground.

"Papa," Martha screamed. "Josie's hurt. Really bad."

Rachel ran and knelt beside the trembling dog. Then she saw. Through Josie's torn-out stomach she saw the dog's intestines, nearly falling out. She lifted her eyes to Martha. "What happened?"

Martha couldn't answer, but shrugged.

Just then Tom Dorland appeared. "What happened?"

"She doesn't know," Rachel answered softly.

Mr. Lawford appeared with a gun in his hand. Leaning over the dog, he talked softly to her. "I'm sorry, Josie," he murmured, "but you're hurt so badly we can't fix you." He lifted the gun and Rachel turned away.

"Don't do it!" Tom Dorland said in a trembling voice. "Please don't do it, Mr. Lawford."

Mr. Lawford lowered the gun and looked into the young doctor's eyes. "Nothin' else to do," he said. "Coyotes got her. She's ripped clean apart." He raised the gun again.

"Let me try to fix her," Tom pleaded. "I don't know if I can save her and she'll have a lot of pain but she might make it."

Mr. Lawford looked at Martha. She nodded. "Yes, I want to save her, Papa. I love Josie."

"I know you do. But it's cruel to put her through the pain when she could die painlessly. She'll die anyway, you know."

Martha shot Tom a pleading look. "Please try, Dr. Dorland. Please save my dog."

The young man swallowed loudly, blinking the moisture from his eyes. "I'll do my best," he choked out. He swallowed again, squared his shoulders, and spoke. "Will someone please take Miss Lawford away for an hour? And I'll need someone else to help me."

Suddenly, Rachel wanted desperately to help Josie. "I'll do it," she said, standing straight and swallowing her tears. "I love Josie more than anyone else. . .except Martha. She'll like having me with her."

"All right," Tom said, opening his case. "We'll try to disinfect the wound with alcohol and it'll burn like fire. Can you hold her?"

Josie lay almost still while Rachel whispered into her ear and Tom poured whiskey over and around her intestines. The pitiful moans caused tears to roll down Rachel's cheeks but she kept up her soft talk and held on tightly.

"Now I'm ready to sew her up," the serious-voiced young doctor said. "How about a man taking Miss Butler's place. Rachel. . .Miss Butler, you help me with the stitching and keep talking to Josie. It really helps. It could make the difference whether she lives or dies."

Andy Shackleford held Josie still while Rachel held the wound closed and talked to Josie until she thought her throat would close up. "Good girl, Josie. Just lie still so the doctor can make you well. I know he's hurting you, baby, but he has to put you back together." Over and over and over.

"Well, I think we're finished," Tom finally said. "You're a fine assistant, Miss Butler." His voice still shook.

Rachel felt so weak she sat on the tongue of the wagon to catch her breath. As she rested, she heard Tom's soft voice.

"Our Dear Father in heaven," he said, barely above a whisper. "We thank You for loving each of us, as well as all Your creation. We just tried to save this special dog's life, Father. We've done the best we know how. We can sew flesh together, but we can't heal, so we're asking You. We ask in Jesus' name and thank You for hearing and answering our prayers. Amen." He turned to the waiting people. "Josie will have to ride in a wagon for some time."

The doctor walked off quietly, bag in hand. He said nothing and no one spoke to him. The enormous lump in Rachel's throat stopped her from saying anything to anyone.

Rachel's father moved to Josie's side. "She can ride in our wagon."

Mr. Lawford very gently lifted Josie up into his arms. "She'll ride in ours," he said. He laid the dog on Martha's featherbed. "Martha will have to find a new place to sleep," he said tenderly to Rachel. "She won't mind."

When Rachel's strength returned, she ran after Martha and her mother. "Josie's all right so far," she told Martha.

The next day Josie still lived and rode in the wagon. Rachel remembered how bumpy it was and wished she could help Josie somehow.

Dr. Dorland joined them for a few minutes that day. "Josie must have plenty of food now," he told Martha. "You feed her all you can spare and I'll bring her something when I can."

As they walked along the road, they saw several more graves and lots of dead animals.

Two days later, they reached the trail that led to Chimney Rock, three miles off the Trail. The train stopped so those who wanted could go see the huge rock formation up close, though it was plainly visible from the Trail.

Dan approached them on his large gelding. "Someone want to ride with me?"

"No," Rachel said with finality. "A horse is never supposed to carry more than ten percent of its own weight. That means one person per horse. We'll ride my family's three horses."

"You're right," Dan said. "But we'll be going only a little way, and we'll go slowly."

"We'll ride my family's horses," Rachel said. The three girls rode the horses, leaving the little boys with the older Lawfords.

As they neared the large Chimney Rock, Dan estimated it to be about 250 feet high, with the chimney on top measuring about 75 feet. The young people climbed up 200 feet and engraved their names in the soft stone, among the myriads of others who'd gone before.

"Look! Indians!" Andy Shackleford yelled as they

climbed down the structure. Rachel raised her eyes to see a dozen Indians, each on a spotted pony, moving toward them. No one had any weapons so they just waited.

"Maybe we should make a break for the wagons," Pastor Richards said.

"No Indians have hurt us yet," Dan said. "I doubt they'll be starting now."

When the Indians reached them, Rachel saw they were young, even younger than she. The Indians smiled and pointed to their bows and quivers of arrows. Then they motioned to the Train's young people as if pulling back bowstrings.

"They want us to shoot," Tom Dorland murmured. In a little while the red youth and white youth engaged in a shooting contest, which the experienced Indians easily won. Waving and smiling, the young Indians rode off the way they'd come.

The young people of the wagon train headed back to the wagons in good spirits, their opinions of Indians up about 500 percent. As the merry group neared the wagon train, they came upon a herd of buffalo a mile wide by the Platte River. Of one accord they all stayed back, fearing the huge animals would stampede and run over them. The buffalo ignored the people on horses, giving them a good chance to enjoy the magnificent creatures.

Later that day Tom Dorland brought Josie a small, skinned animal. "I'll try to do this often," he told Martha.

The next day they reached Scott's Bluff, 596 miles from home, with many 500-foot-tall bluffs. The crystal clear sky opened up the landscape until it looked as if you could see forever.

"The guidebook says you can see three hundred miles," Papa said.

"I'm sure I can see that far," Martha said laughing.

"What about you boys?"

"I can see all the way to Heaven," Willie said.

Petey gave Willie a big push, sending him sprawling. "No you can't. That's straight up in the sky."

Tears trickled down Willie's face, then a sob burst from his throat. Martha gathered him into her arms and carried him a while.

"You're a bad boy," Rachel said to Petey. "You made Willie cry. Don't you know he's smaller than you?"

Martha soon had Willie laughing and set him down. She dropped an arm over Petey's shoulder. "You didn't mean to hurt Willie, did you?" she asked the small boy. He leaned against her, putting his cheek on her arm.

One evening a high wind arose, bringing heavy rain. Before long the wagons were in danger of being blown over.

"Call the boys," Debbie Petty yelled and right away Tom Dorland, Dan Barlow, Andy Shackleford, George Rahn, Nate Butler, and George Lawford showed up. "Let's fasten all the wagons together," Debbie yelled into the wind.

"Good idea," Nate Butler replied. Working quickly in the wind and rain, they fastened them together so they couldn't tip over.

"Good," Tom Dorland screamed into the wind. "But that won't keep the contents dry. I guess everyone's on his own now."

Rachel's wagon leaked but it was better than being in the rain. And it felt so much better having the wagons more secure.

The next morning the sun shone brightly and wildflowers bloomed everywhere. After everyone dried the contents of their wagons, they marched onward. And saw more graves.

The train traveled among the gigantic bluffs for several days.

"At least they protect us from the wind," Rachel said to Martha while looking up at the mountainous bluffs around them.

One day as they walked, Josie whined from Martha's wagon. "She wants to walk," Martha said. "She's been begging for several days. Think she should?"

Rachel ran to the head of the wagon line to find Dr. Dorland. "Josie wants to walk," she said. "Can she?"

"For one hour," he said. "You might also tell Miss Lawford that I'm planning to take out the stitches tonight."

Mr. Lawford lifted the dog down and Josie obviously enjoyed herself though walking gingerly. Later, when Martha's father put her back into the wagon, she barked her disapproval.

That evening Tom Dorland stopped by Rachel's wagon. "Come help me take out Josie's stitches," he said. "It wouldn't be fair if I didn't ask you," he added, "as this is the fun part."

When Martha brought Josie out to Tom, the dog began trembling hard. She squatted low and her tail dropped to the ground.

Tom knelt beside her and put his arms around her, talking softly. "I hurt you badly last time, didn't I, girl? I don't blame you for being afraid." He smiled. "But I'm not going to hurt you at all this time." He raised his eyes to Rachel. "Come and hold her."

Rachel dropped to the ground and turned Josie over so her stomach was exposed. She could hardly believe how much better the dog looked. Hardly any swelling, hardly any redness, and the wound itself under the stitches looked dry and black. "It's all right," she whispered to the still-trembling dog. "We're going to be very careful with you, Josie, and make you all well." She couldn't believe the love she felt for the shaggy dog.

She talked to Josie as Tom worked swiftly but gently. "There you go," he said about two minutes later. He petted the big head. "Doesn't that feel better? Now it won't pull anymore, Josie." He lifted his head to Rachel. "Thanks, Miss Butler. Some day you're going to be a nurse." Then he got to his feet and turned to Martha, who'd been standing near, watching fearfully.

"She's just fine, Miss Lawford. Much better than I could have hoped. She's a good patient, too. Did you notice she didn't flinch once?"

Martha shook her head. "No, but I'll never be able to tell you how much Josie and I appreciate what you did. I love her so much, Dr. Dorland."

He laughed quietly. "Call me Tom. And I can see how much you love her. But don't thank me. I can't heal anyone or anything. God does His miracle every time any wound heals, no matter how small. In Josie's case it was a big miracle. God created animals, too, and He loves them even more than you do. She'd have never made it without His special care. Did you ever think of that?"

Martha's smile held a beautiful radiance. Rachel felt jealousy rise in her throat. "I didn't think of it," Martha answered, "but now that I do, I know you're right." She raised her beautiful blue eyes to the cloudless sky. "Thank You, Father. Thank You so much for loving and healing Josie. I love You."

Tom's eyes softened. "You really do, don't you?" He turned back to Rachel. "Thanks again for the help, Miss Butler." He picked up his black case and headed off among the wagons.

Martha's eyes still radiated love. "Isn't he wonderful?" she said quietly.

"Yes," Rachel agreed. "He's a good doctor." Sometimes she wished she had the faith of these two good people.

The next day they met more turnarounds, as they called the men returning from the Trail.

"There's so many dead animals ahead you won't be able to go on," one of the dirty, tattered men said. "They're in the Trail, beside the Trail, and even all through the streams. The smell makes you sick and the water'll kill you."

True to the men's word, each day rotting carcasses became more prevalent, and the smell truly made Rachel sick. She could hardly face food. One day she happened to take a look at her body and discovered that all the plumpness had disappeared. She looked hard and lean. Smiling, she decided not everything on Heartbreak Trail was bad. Not quite everything.

A few days later they crossed over the Laramie River on a shaky bridge that the Indians had made. They charged two dollars per wagon which everyone paid rather than ford the river. When the train made camp to prepare for the Sabbath, Indians swarmed everywhere, most of them dressed in white man's tattered clothing. A few wore buckskins. All wore soft moccasins.

Rachel and Martha always did their families' washings now. "Want to help me do Sandy Piling's?" Martha always asked. Rachel usually said no, but this time she took half and they finished it in another hour.

The next morning, May eighth, was the Sabbath. Pastor Richards conducted a moving hymn sing early in the morning. With his lovely voice and pleasant way of getting everyone into the spirit, the music bathed the prairie in happy and joyful sound. Rachel felt herself growing close to God and she had no intention of doing that.

Then he preached about how much God loves each person. "He loves us much more than any earthly parents ever loved their own child," he said. "God actually loves us as much as He loves His precious only Son. We know because He allowed his Son to die for our sins so we could live with Him forever."

Rachel had always heard about "God so loved the world" but she'd never really thought about how much God loved her.

At dinner time Julia, Martha, and Rachel found their own little spot to spread their blanket to enjoy the meal together. Not that there was any special food. Everyone brought beans fixed one way or another and people had made cakes or dried-apple pies the best they could. But they enjoyed relaxing together.

As the girls filled their plates, Petey ran to them. "Can I eat with you, Martha?" he asked. "I'll be good."

Martha pulled him close. "Of course you can, Petey. Do you have a dish and spoon?" He ran back after them.

When the girls returned to their blanket, they discovered another one a few feet from theirs. "Shall we go somewhere else?" Rachel asked.

"No," Martha said. "Maybe God wants us to meet some new friends today. There are many people on the train we don't know."

Dan Barlow appeared with a huge plate of food and sat down on the blanket. Rachel checked Julia's face and found excitement all over it. That girl really liked Dan.

# eight

Before Dan looked in the girls' direction, Pastor Richards, Tom Dorland, and Andy Shackleford arrived with heaping plates and dropped to the blanket. "Ah," the preacher said. "Does this feel good or does this feel good?"

"It feels good," Tom said. Then his eyes happened on the girls. "Hey, fellows!" he said with excitement. "Look who followed us here." The others looked the ten feet to the girls and showed surprise, too.

A big laugh burst from Rachel's throat. "You didn't even notice our quilt, did you?"

"No," Dan said. "Was it there?" He shook his light-colored head. "No. Why don't you girls just admit you couldn't resist eating with us?"

"I admit it," Julia said, laughing too. "We put our blanket here so we could eat with you."

Dan moved over a little and patted the quilt beside him. His clear eyes drilled into Julia's. "Is that a fact? In that case, why don't you prove it. Come over here and sit with me. Please?"

Julia picked up her plate, marched over, and sat beside Dan, then smiled a "see what I did" smile at Rachel and Martha.

Half a second later Pastor Richards heaved his six-foot-plus frame to his feet, carefully lifted his overflowing plate, and headed toward the girls' blanket. At last! Rachel had been waiting a long time for this. She moved over slightly to make room for him. But he walked around the blanket and dropped to the quilt beside Martha. For a moment

Rachel thought she'd cry, but she swallowed twice and hid her disappointment. Just then Andy Shackleford dropped beside her.

"Well, here I am, odd man out," Dr. Dorland said.

Immediately, Petey got up and carefully carried his half-filled plate to the men's quilt and sat beside the doctor. "I'll be with you," Petey said. "Willie's eating with his mama and papa so I don't have anyone, either."

Tom patted Petey's shoulder. "We'll get along fine, won't we Petey? Pretty soon we'll go back and get some cake or pie."

Later in the afternoon the talk turned to God and how they could know His will for them.

"God doesn't care for any of us," Rachel said loudly. "Would a God Who cares let His people go through what's been happening to us? Not to mention the animals. How could He let the animals suffer and die when they didn't do anything to deserve it? And little kids! God doesn't care!" When she finally stopped, the silence went on forever. She wanted to demand that the preacher answer her accusations, but she refused to talk to him because he chose to sit with Martha.

Rachel had put such a pall over the group that they soon broke up and went to their separate wagons. Later that night Rachel wondered if she'd made a major mistake. A minister might want a real Christian for a good friend . . .or especially for a wife.

The next day they reached Fort Laramie, 650 miles from home, the second fort set up to guard the Oregon Trail. The fort looked nearly like Fort Kearney, big, ugly, and adobe. Beyond the fort lay a little city of neat white houses. Rachel would have liked to walk among the houses and feel a tiny bit civilized but Captain Ransom hurried them on.

As they bought provisions, the officer told Nate and others that '59 was the largest migration ever known. "Over thirteen hundred wagons have been past here already," he said, "and twelve-hundred-head of herded cattle."

When they returned to their wagons, Nate laughed. "Did you hear the man say thirteen hundred wagons are ahead of us," he said to Alma and Rachel. "And we thought we were in one of the earliest trains."

They hadn't gone far when the wagon ruts grew deeper. They'd seen deep ruts but nothing like these. Pretty soon word filtered down the wagon line that this place was called Register Cliffs and had the deepest ruts on the entire Trail. Cliffs on each side of the Trail got taller as they traveled. The wagons had to go single file because of the cliffs and the ruts soon reached the middle of the oxen's bodies.

Rachel began to feel crowded as she, Martha, Julia, Petey, and Willie walked single file beside the wagons. When Dan Barlow came along, he and Julia messed around until the others left them. Soon, Petey and Willie got cross and so did Rachel. The cliffs on each side made Rachel feel as if she were in a small world and couldn't get her breath.

"This is the worst ever," Rachel complained to Martha. "I can't stand this anymore."

"It isn't so bad," Martha answered. "It's a lot better than the deep sand. The oxen had bad trouble in that."

Rachel knew Martha was right but she didn't say it out loud. "Well, it's always too hot or too cold," she said, "and too dusty or windy. Or something else."

"But this isn't so bad," Martha insisted. "The oxen are doing all right and the temperature is comfortable."

"Why do you always have to be so perfect?" Rachel

snapped. "Do you have any idea how tiresome that gets?"

Martha crumpled a little. "No," she said in a tiny voice. "I was just trying to cheer you up. I want you to know God loves you, Rachel, and is taking care of you."

"God doesn't love me! He doesn't love you either. You just keep saying that to keep your courage up."

After a short silence Martha spoke in a tiny voice. "Do you believe there is a God, Rachel?"

That surprised Rachel a lot. She couldn't deny she believed that. She nodded.

"Do you believe the Bible is God's Word? And that it is true?"

Rachel bowed her head. "Yes," she mumbled.

Martha looked as if she'd just been given a fine gift. "If you believe the Bible's true," she said, "you have to believe God loves you. It says He loves you as much as if you were His only child. Remember Pastor Richards said God loves you more than you can love your own children. That means He loves you much more than your father and mother love you. Many times more, Rachel. Did you know He loves you so much He cries when you reject Him?"

Rachel couldn't answer Martha anymore, but her friend's words hung in her mind. God loved her more than her parents do? Papa had brought her on this long Heartbreak Trail against her wishes but she knew both her parents loved her with all their hearts. She was everything to her parents. And God loved her more than that?

That night, as she lay on her comfortable featherbed, she thought about it some more. God loved her many times more than her parents did. Martha had said that was because He loved sinlessly, a perfect love, and her folk's love was a selfish love. All human love is selfish because all have sinned.

As she lay there she felt love for Him grow in her heart until she could hardly contain it all. She felt happier than she could ever remember feeling in her whole entire life.

The next day she asked Martha some questions. "I've gone to church all my life," she said, "but I don't have any idea how to know Jesus as you do."

"It's purely easy," Martha said. "Just tell Him how much you love Him, and that you want to love Him more. Thank Him for dying to pay for everything you've ever done wrong, tell Him you want to become His child, and ask Him to forgive your sins. That's it, Rachel. That's all there is to it." Martha choked on the last two short sentences, as though she were about to burst into tears.

"Aren't you glad I want to do this?" Rachel asked.

Martha hugged Rachel. "I'm so happy I'm crying," she blubbered against Rachel's cheek. "Now, do it."

"I love You, God," Rachel cried. "I love You because You love me so much, enough to die for me. Thank You for loving me so much. Thank You for dying for my sins. Please, God, I want to belong to You! Forgive my sins and teach me how to be Your child." She stopped and sniffed. Then she coughed. "I love You, God," she sobbed.

"I love Him, too," Petey said. "Can I be His child?"

"Me too," Willie echoed. "I love Jesus, too."

Martha stopped right there in that narrow alley between the high cliffs and hugged them both. "You're both His very own little boys," she said to them. "You must always remember that, no matter what. All right?"

"Let's sing," Rachel suggested. So the little boy voices joined the girls' as familiar hymns rang out from their hearts.

The wagon train soon camped along Horseshoe Creek, not getting very far due to the ruts, cliffs, and bluffs. They found plenty of grass and water for the animals and wood for the fires.

As they traveled, they saw more and more graves as well as animal carcasses along the Trail. They also met turnarounds nearly every day. They all told of the same dire future for the wagon train.

By the time they reached the Laramie Mountains with snow on the mountain tops, the sun was scorching.

"I'm hot," Willie said one day. "I need a drink, Martha. Please, get me a drink."

"I can't, Willie. We have to wait until we stop tonight."

"I can't wait. I'm thirsty now."

"So am I," Petey said. "My throat hurts."

"Why don't we pretend we're in a nice cool lake, swimming," Rachel said. "The water comes to our shoulders so we just lie down and start kicking our legs and stroking with our hands. Are you getting too cold, Willie?"

Willie laughed with delight at the game. "Not yet," he said. "I want to swim some more."

"All right," Rachel said. "Just be careful you don't go out too far. It might get deep."

Both boys got into the game until they forgot all about being hot and thirsty.

The next day when the boys napped, Rachel wanted desperately to do something for God. "Martha," she said. "How can I let God know how much I love Him? I just want to show Him."

"You showed Him yesterday," she said. "When you took the boys swimming you showed God your love. The Bible says, if you do something nice for anyone, even the least, it's as if you did it for the Lord. So just look around. There are lots of people on the train who need help. And helping them will make you feel better than you ever have. It's really doing it for Him, Rachel."

Rachel watched but didn't see anything special she

could do.

The next afternoon the train stopped for some reason. A few minutes later, Rachel heard a woman crying loudly. When Rachel went to see what was wrong, she found Tom Dorland talking softly to Tamara Richards. As he talked, Rachel realized a snake had just bitten the woman. The doctor kept reassuring the terrified woman but he didn't do anything. Why doesn't he get to it? Rachel wondered. The woman will die if he doesn't do something.

Suddenly, Rachel had a strong feeling that she should help the preacher's sister. She walked up to them. "May I help you, doctor?" she asked.

Relief washed over his face when he looked up. "Please do," he said. "I just prayed for someone to come, and He sent you." He showed her how to loosen the tourniquet he'd placed on the woman's swollen arm. "I'll tell you when," he said. "In the meantime I have to incise the wounds. Will you hold the arm still for me?"

When they finished the grizzly job, Rachel cradled Tamara's head in her arms for a moment. "I'm sorry we hurt you," she whispered. "But now you're going to get well."

Tom thanked Rachel and told her he'd be calling on her again. "You really should be a nurse," he added with a sincere smile.

Rachel, in a rosy glow, hurried back to her wagon. Martha had been right. She felt better then she ever had.

The wagon train resumed its journey and, after a while, they came to a ferry. But, since the river didn't look deep, they decided to ford it. As they forced the animals into the river though, the animals refused to cross. After many of the animals refused several times, the people paid the money and ferried everything across—wagons, animals, and people.

"I ain't lettin' these critters tell me what to do," Mark Piling said, wielding his whip. He drove his animals into the water many times but each time they turned back. Finally, he spurred his horse into the water, too, and whipped the oxen pulling the wagon, ripping strips of flesh from their bodies. His screaming and the oxen's loud bawling got the attention of the entire wagon train who gathered on the other side of the river to watch.

"Let them go back," Nate yelled. "I'll pay your ferry, Piling. Don't force them across."

If Piling heard he didn't respond. Finally, the bleeding oxen struggled out of the water, the wagon bumping up the river bank behind them. He drove them on about thirty feet, then turned back to drive his stock across. He had one milk cow, twelve horses, and four more oxen.

Forcing them all into the water together he continued using the whip harshly on their backs. The horse he rode tried desperately to turn back too, but Piling spurred him until he screamed. This time when the animals reached the current, the cow spun a complete circle then, at the mercy of the cruel water, washed downstream, sometimes her head out of the water, sometimes her feet out. Two of the horses lost control and the river swept them away, too. When the other horses and oxen made it across, they climbed wearily out on the other side. Piling followed them on his horse, pushing it to go faster. They nearly made it to the edge when an undercurrent swept his mount's feet out from under it, spilling the man into the stream. The horse disappeared downstream in the frothy water. Piling managed to stay on top of the water but hurtled downstream until he disappeared.

"Well, so much for that," Captain Ransom said. "Who's gonna tell his woman?"

# nine

No one offered to tell Sandra Piling that the river had swept her husband away.

"Shall we?" Martha whispered into Rachel's ear. "We probably know her better than anyone. . .from doing her washing."

Everything in Rachel shouted for her to get out of there before Martha talked her into doing something she'd be sorry about. "Let's go," she heard a strained voice say, then recognized it to be her own. How could she do this? She'd just caught herself thinking that it served the horrible man right. He'd caused the death of several helpless animals. Why shouldn't he die, too? She shook her head. That wasn't good thinking. God would never have her think that way. *Help me, God,* she prayed as she followed Martha.

The Piling wagon was only a few feet away. Maybe Mrs. Piling had heard the commotion and already knew. Rachel jumped up onto the wagon behind Martha.

"Are you all right, Mrs. Piling?" Martha asked in her soft sweet voice.

Mrs. Piling sat up in her rough bed on the floor of the wagon. "Yes. Is something wrong?"

Tears reddened Martha's eyes. She nodded and took the woman's hand. "Yes. The river just swept your husband away. I'm afraid he's gone, Mrs. Piling."

The frail woman smiled. "Thank you, dear. Now, don't worry about me. I'm all right." Rachel thought for sure she saw relief in the woman's face. No, she must have imagined it.

"Can we do anything for you?" Martha asked.

The woman thought a moment. "I'll need a little time to get organized," she said. "Do you think I can drive the oxen?"

Martha's dark head swung back and forth. "Driving's a hard job, Mrs. Piling. A sick person could never do it. The men will think of something."

"Let me try before you get anyone else. I think I can do it."

"All right. We'll camp here tonight so you can get yourself together."

As the girls hurried back to their wagons, Rachel voiced to Martha her thoughts about Mrs. Piling showing relief at her husband's death.

"Don't even think such things," Martha scolded, "let alone say them."

Captain Ransom gladly made camp. "You be sure to see what we can do for her," he told Martha and Rachel.

The two girls returned to the Piling wagon just before dark. Rachel brought some fresh milk and cream that was getting more dear every day. The cows had cut from thirty gallons a day to about six. They found Mrs. Piling up and caring for her children.

"Would you like us to take the children for tonight?" Martha asked.

The woman's eyes, looking brighter than Rachel had ever seen them, looked up from the fire she cooked over. "Oh no," she said in a strong clear voice. "We're doing just fine. We'll stay together, but thanks anyway." She handed Petey a plate of bacon and pancakes swimming in brown syrup.

As they approached their own wagons again, Rachel didn't say a word, but she'd never seen Sandy Piling look so strong and happy. She wasn't imagining it, either.

A little later Tom Dorland stopped at Rachel's wagon. "Could you go with me to see Sandra Piling?" he asked. "In her condition a blow like this could be very hard on her." Rachel kept quiet but gladly went.

Tom listened to the woman's heart and lungs and did some other things, then smiled broadly. "You're doing just fine, Mrs. Piling. Just fine. If you get anxious or feel bad, don't hesitate to call me. Please accept our condolences. We're so very sorry."

As Tom walked Rachel back to her wagon, she hoped he'd say something. Sandra's relief had been as plain as the rising sun. But he didn't mention Mrs. Piling at all.

Early the next morning Rachel took a pot of oatmeal with cream floating on it to the Piling wagon. Rachel dropped the oatmeal and nearly fainted when Mark Piling himself jumped down from the wagon and met her belligerently. "My family don't need your charity," he snapped when he saw the pot.

Rachel didn't say a word, just grabbed her empty oatmeal pot and ran for her parents' wagon. "Mama, Mama!" she called. When her mother appeared, she continued. "Mark Piling's back. Oh Mama, why couldn't he stay dead?"

"Rachel!" Mama cried in distress. "I thought you were doing so well and now this! How could you say such a thing, young lady? And are you sure he's back? That he didn't drown."

"He didn't, Mama, and he's as mean as ever." Then Rachel couldn't help it. She told her mother how happy Sandy had been when she thought her husband dead. "She got right out of bed, Mama, and she was all well."

"I've heard about situations like that, Rachel. She might be better off without him, but he doesn't have to die."

Word soon got around that Piling was alive and as nasty as ever. Rachel wanted to go see Sandra Piling to see how she was now, but her mean husband kept people away as he always had.

"Are you happy your daddy's back?" she couldn't help asking Petey that morning. The little boy hung his head and wouldn't answer.

That day they traveled in a continuous line of wagon trains; where one ended the next began. And the dust was terrible. Sometimes they couldn't see their own oxen. Everyone's eyes burned as they choked on the terrible dry stuff.

Late in the afternoon word came to Rachel that Andy Shackleford was sick, possibly with cholera. The Ransoms had taken him into their wagon.

That night there was nothing to burn but sagebrush. It burned fast, not putting out much heat, and the smell sickened Rachel's stomach.

The train stayed in camp the next day as Tom Dorland didn't think Andy should bounce around in a wagon.

That afternoon, several cows got into some quicksand by the river. Tom, Dan, Nate, George Lawford, George Rahn, Debbie Petty, and three other men ran to the scene with ropes. Tom, being the lightest, ran to the cattle and fastened them together. Then the men pulled on the ropes while Tom urged the animals to struggle. It looked as if they'd go down. Rachel wanted to run and help but she didn't. Finally, the valiant animals started to move. The men cheered and pulled harder. Within an hour they had them all out. Every one.

The next day they stayed in camp again. Andy seemed a bit better but one of Thurman Tate's oxen died. Someone discovered rabbits and sage hens in and around the sagebrush. Jackson Lawford and others went out and brought back enough for several meals for their families.

As Martha and Rachel cleaned their meat, they saw a man go hunting without a gun.

"I ain't got one," he answered when they asked him about it. "But I'll catch something anyways." He soon found a rabbit and chased it all around the camp and through sagebrush. He ran until he dropped, exhausted.

Although Martha and Rachel laughed at his antics, they gave him two cleaned sage hens.

On Sunday, May fifteenth, Rachel got to sleep later but still wasn't ready to awaken when Captain Ransom came around.

"We have to move on," he told everyone. "The cattle have eaten all the grass and they need all they can get."

"How's Andy?"

"Not good. I hate to move him but we have to care for the cattle, too."

They left the Platte for the last time and camped near Willow Springs. After supper Rachel saw Tom Dorland head for Ransom's wagon. "May I help you with Andy?" she asked.

He shook his head. "I'd rather you stayed away. I'm sure it's cholera and somehow it gets around. No need for you to chance getting it."

"What about you?"

The doctor shrugged. "Someone has to take care of him. But truthfully, there isn't much a person can do for cholera."

As Rachel walked away, she looked back and saw Tom praying over Andy. A black dread covered her. Andy might die. What a horrible thought! Andy really might die!

Later, Tom asked Rachel to help him dress Tamara

Richard's snake bite wounds. The woman looked good and her wounds were healing nicely.

The next day they saw the Sweetwater Mountains with ice and snow glistening on the peaks. When Petey and Willie complained about being too hot, Rachel showed them the cool tops of the mountains.

"The white on them is ice and snow," she said. "We'll pretend the cold is down here." She shivered and hugged her arms to her chest. "Brrrr. I'm cold," she whined. "Willie, would you run and get me a sweater, please?"

"No," Petey interrupted, thrilled with the game. "You have to be cold because you don't have a sweater."

"All right. I guess I'll get warm next summer when the sun comes out."

The sight of the cool mountaintops kept the boys cool the rest of the day.

"You're getting good with the boys," Martha told her. "You're really helping 'the least of these,' Rachel."

Rachel laughed happily. "I discovered you're right. It feels good to help and be kind to people."

One day they met a small train of four wagons. "You're going the wrong way," Julia called when they met.

The oxen driver stopped his wagon. "You're right," he called back. "We're taking seventeen children back to civilization. Indians massacred all the adults in their train and left the children."

Rachel could hardly bear to listen anymore. What was in store for them? Would they ever get to Oregon? Were the same Indians lying in wait for them?

On Sunday, May twenty-second, before the preaching service began, Dan took Julia from Martha and Rachel and found a place for them to sit. Afterward, the group put their food together as usual. The girls had barely started filling their plates when Pastor Richards came and asked Martha to eat with him.

"We'd be glad to, wouldn't we, Rachel?"

Rachel's first inclination was to stick her nose in the air and flounce away, but better sense told her this would be an opportunity to impress the minister. So, she held her tongue.

Pastor Richards gave his attention so completely to Martha he barely knew Rachel was there. "Did you like my sermon today?" he asked her.

"Oh, yes," Martha said. "I always love to hear about our Lord."

"I mean the wording, and the way I delivered it."

"Oh, dear," Martha wailed, "I listened so hard to what you said about my Jesus I forgot to notice how you said it."

"Oh. Well, did you enjoy my song leading?"

"The only thing I like better than singing to our God is praying to Him," she said with a silvery laugh.

"I see. Well, did I look presentable?"

Martha laughed heartily at that. "You always look nice, reverend. How you do it, I can't guess. Everyone else looks like a strong gale just dropped them."

He laughed in appreciation. "I thought it was a minister's duty to look presentable at all times. Do you like the way I wear my hair?"

By this time Rachel began to wonder if the pastor's charm included his good looks and nothing else. She'd never heard anyone so vain in her life. Then her conscience told her she was having a bad case of sour grapes. Maybe. Oh, but he was good looking. She felt like laughing out loud as Martha struggled for diplomatic answers to the man's inane questions.

"I don't notice hair," Martha said softly. "I notice

willing workers in an emergency, people out helping others, and I especially enjoy being with people who love to talk about our Lord."

Rachel smiled to herself when Pastor Richards had the grace to blush. Martha's words probably hurt him a lot. Everything she'd mentioned, he lacked. After gulping a few breaths of air, the minister smiled. "Well, know what I enjoy? I enjoy being with you. Know why? Because you're sweet and dear, and one hundred percent honest even if it hurts." He squirmed a moment before continuing. "Now, how about you two lovely ladies going for a little walk with me?"

"I'd like that," Martha said, "but I promised Mama I'd take care of Willie while she takes a nap."

The fine looking head turned Rachel's way. Suddenly, she didn't yearn to be with him as much as she had. But she couldn't be sure. "I'd enjoy that," she said.

They walked through the sagebrush away from the wagon train, causing several rabbits to scurry away.

"If it weren't the Sabbath I'd get you some meat," he said to Rachel.

"I'm glad it's Sabbath then," she said. "Don't you feel bad having to hurt innocent animals?"

He jerked his eyes open in surprise. "I hadn't thought about it," he said.

"You hadn't? Don't you know they get scared and feel pain just like we do? And when you shoot an animal it may leave a nest of babies to starve."

He slowed to a stroll as he considered Rachel's words. Finally, he shook his head. "No, I don't think so. They aren't smart enough to be scared and I doubt they feel much, either."

"Why do you suppose they run so fast from men?"

He looked perplexed. "I don't know." Then a smile

reached from his full lips to his dark, deep-fringed eyes. Rachel's heart nearly missed a beat as she took in the tall, extremely handsome man. "But," the minister continued, "don't confuse me with the facts, all right? You could ruin one of my greatest pleasures—eating."

By unspoken agreement they turned back toward the wagons. "How would you like to think up a subject for me to preach about next week?" he asked as they walked.

"I'd like that," she said quickly before he changed his mind. "And I have the subject already. I'd like for you to tell the people exactly how to accept our Lord Jesus' great sacrifice for us and be saved."

His dark eyebrows lifted ever so slightly. "Everyone already knows that."

"Don't be so sure. You should teach that every few months forever."

By this time, they'd reached the wagons. "Thanks for walking with me," he said. "I'll give your suggestion some thought."

Later in the afternoon, Tom came to Rachel's wagon. "I wondered if you could go with me to check Tamara Richards one more time. I'm sure she's fine but I need to be sure, for her sake as well as mine."

The woman's wounds were almost healed but she was glad to see Tom and Rachel. "My brother James doesn't stay around much," she said, "and I get lonely."

"There's someone who could really use a friend," Tom said as they walked back to the Butler wagons.

Tom didn't stop long enough to tell her how to go about the good deed he'd suggested. Rachel wondered how she could befriend Tamara Richards, or if she wanted to.

The next day they passed Alkali Lake, an evil-smelling body of water many miles long. The water had an ugly whitish cast but the hot thirsty animals tried hard to reach it. The drivers held them back as the guidebook said the water was poisonous. The many dead animals lying along the Trail reminded everyone to restrain their animals, no matter what. Graves grew more numerous each day, too. The Trail was definitely taking its toll.

Soon, they came to Independence Rock, 815 miles from Independence. The huge granite rock, 500 feet long, 200 feet wide, and 250 feet tall stood alone in the Sweetwater Valley. Rachel, Martha, and Julia all grabbed knives, planning to carve their names in the Rock but soon learned granite isn't soft like Chimney Rock had been. The many names on the rock hadn't been carved in but painted on. They gave up and ran to catch up with the train.

Later that afternoon Tom Dorland stopped the train to tell them Andy Shackleford had died. Pastor Richards spoke a few words then they buried him right in the Trail. Rachel thought that was awful, but when the wagons started running over the grave she burst into tears.

# ten

"We run the wagons over the grave so animals or Indians won't recognize the grave and dig it up," Tom, who'd come up behind her, explained. "It looks awful but it's for protection."

Rachel felt black depression after Andy died. Why did the people and animals keep dying? And for nothing! Right now she hated Heartbreak Trail more than she could say.

Martha talked to her all the rest of the day. "You feel God's love for you don't you?" she asked quietly.

Rachel nodded and swiped at her running nose with the back of her hand. "I thought I did."

"Don't allow yourself to doubt His love. Not for a minute, even when hard things come. We can't hope to understand everything, but we can trust and love. Then He'll help us through. Here's something else to think about. God loves Andy more than we did. Even more than his mother and father did. Many times more, so we just have to trust Him to make good come from bad."

After some time Rachel started to feel better. She needed to feel better for the little boys' sakes anyway. She started a game with them and by the time they camped, she felt His love again. Although she felt sad for Andy she truly knew God loved and cared for him forever.

They forded the Sweetwater River the next morning. The river was cold and clear, sixty feet wide and three feet deep. The stifling hot weather tempted the girls to wade across.

"Think we can?" Martha asked in response to Rachel's suggestion.

"The book says it's three feet deep," Rachel said. "We'll have to carry the boys partway but we can do that."

All the walkers in the train ended up wading across and having a wonderful time doing it. It cooled them for several hours.

A few days later they started up the Rocky Mountains on good but steep roads. Another of Mark Piling's oxen gave out and they left it lying on the ground.

"Who's going to take care of it?" Petey asked.

Rachel shuddered. "We'll pray for God to help it get well," she told him and they did. Rachel left the ox, hoping desperately that God would heal it.

Soon the roads became insufferably dusty. As a result, everyone's eyes became inflamed and sore. Some people had goggles to wear over their eyes, others wore veils. Martha and Rachel had only linen handkerchiefs so they tied them around their faces and also the little boys' faces.

Later the same day, Rachel had an idea. "Martha!" she said, "I'm going to cover our oxen's eyes with thin handkerchiefs." But when she tried, the oxen didn't understand she was trying to help them and neither did the drivers. They yelled for her to get out of the way and not to come back, tomorrow or the next day or ever!

A few days later Thurman Tate came past the walking girls, herding a brown cow in front of him. "See what I found," he said proudly. "I can add her to my others and have a herd."

"Does it give milk?" Willie asked.

Tate laughed. "I don't know yet. The thing won't let me get close enough to find out. But I'll get her tamed and breed her in Oregon. First thing you know, I'll have a whole herd of Jerseys."

On Sunday morning, May twenty-ninth, Rachel felt the fierce winds as she lay in bed. The top of the wagon snapped so hard she feared it would tear off the wagon and the cold reached through her many quilts right to her bones. When she finally crawled out of bed, she discovered the wind had brought thick dust with it.

Mama and Rachel had a tough time getting a fire going and when it finally caught, the smoke and dust burned her throat all the way down. How could she endure this for the rest of the summer?

Before they had breakfast ready two men came to talk to Papa. "Why should we stay here?" one of them asked him. "Let's get out of this foul weather."

"I'm not the man to talk to," Papa said. "Go see Captain Ransom, but we agreed to rest on the Sabbath, you know. Maybe we should have faith that the Lord will still the storm. He can, you know."

"Yeah," the man said as they walked away. "But I ain't seen Him doin' it."

About an hour later three wagons left the circle, leaving seventeen wagons and forty-one people.

Thurman Tate came along, looking for his cow. "I guess the wind spooked her," he said. "But I'll find her. I guarantee I'll get her, dead or alive."

The wind and dust continued so strongly that the preaching services and potluck dinner were canceled. So, Rachel ate and slept; she hadn't realized how tired she'd become. Later in the day the wind and dust died down, the sky cleared, and the sun peeked through, giving the travelers a hint of the heat it could still pour onto them.

That evening Tate went looking for his cow again. "I'll get her, you just wait and see," he told Rachel's father. Later, they heard the report of a gun and figured he'd found the cow. Now at least he'd have meat. But Tate came back herding the badly limping cow. "I got her," he yelled at Nate. "Had to shoot her a little but it cooled her down."

"Papa, make him kill her quick," Rachel said, as the cow staggered along in front of Tate.

"Better kill the poor thing and get it over with," Papa called to Tate.

"I ain't killin' her yet, Butler. We'll need the meat more later."

"But that's horrible," Rachel yelled. "Can't you imagine how you'd feel if you were all shot up and someone forced you to go on walking?"

Tate laughed. "I didn't force her to run off."

That night the wind came up again. The wagon rocked until Rachel wondered if it would tip over. The top snapped loudly, almost sounding like the report of guns. Rachel finally asked God to help her sleep, and He did.

The next morning, all of them lightened their loads some more. They broke up trunks for wood and threw out extra axles, shovels, chains, and other things beside the Trail. As the drivers forced their tired oxen on, Rachel, Martha, Julia, Petey, and Willie noticed deserted wagons and carts as well as furniture lining the road. Dead animals lay on and around the castoffs.

Rachel and Martha watched Thurman Tate's oxen stumbling along. When they faltered too much he laid the whip on their backs. He'd tied the cow to the wagon and she staggered along the best she could, bawling at nearly every step.

Rachel went to find Tom Dorland as he felt sympathy for animals more than anyone she knew.

"I'll talk to him," Tom said when Rachel told him about Tate's animals. "But I doubt he'll listen. I haven't heard him listen to anyone yet."

He rode up to Tate's wagon. "Your oxen are looking bad," he said. "Want some help dumping your stuff?"

"Them oxen are all right!" Tate yelled. "Why don't you go put a bandage on your mouth?"

"How about letting me treat the cow then? I might be able to make her more comfortable. She'd heal up faster, too."

"That cow's going to be meat in a week or so, so don't worry about her. You take care of your horse and I'll take care of my livestock."

Tom kept beside the Tate wagon as it moved slowly along. "Well, if you need some help, be sure to ask." Touching his heels to his horse's side he moved ahead.

Rachel stomped along, fuming. "Did you hear that?" she asked Martha.

" 'Most everyone in the train heard it," Martha said. "Calm down, Rachel. You have to learn to accept things you can't change."

Two days later the wagon train reached South Pass. Captain Ransom called the men to a meeting. Thirty minutes later, just as Alma and Rachel had dinner ready, Nate returned with Stan Latham. After they asked God to bless the food and also them, they filled their plates.

"This is where Sublette cutoff leaves the main trail," Nate explained. "It's supposed to save four days travel but there's a fifty-mile stretch with no food or water for the animals."

Rachel turned her back on him and dipped a biscuit into her beans. "What did you decide, Papa?"

Nate grinned through a mouthful of beans. "Well, most of us decided to stay on the main trail. Our animals are gettin' thin and worn. We decided it'd be too hard on them."

"Good for you, dear," Alma said. "You made the right decision."

"But that's not the end of the story. Tate's taking the cutoff. Said he'd wait for us at the other end."

"Oh, Papa, his oxen are worse than anyone's. And you know about his cow."

"I know. But we can't tell the man what to do."

But later that night Tate fixed part of the problem himself. Rachel heard a gunshot a half-hour before Tate appeared. "Want some beef?" he asked. "Just butchered the old cow. Figured she wouldn't make it through the cutoff."

"You figured right," Nate said. "Your oxen won't make it either. Better dump the heavy stuff and still take the regular trail."

Tate said a few words that didn't harmonize too well with his Christian claims. "Do you want some beef or not?" he added.

"I suppose we could use some," Nate said after a little thought.

"Come and get it then," Tate said, marching off. "Seems like people would appreciate some meat way out here," he mumbled.

"I don't want any of his meat," Rachel said. "I won't eat it either."

Nate glanced at Alma who shook her head. "Go tell him then," he told Rachel.

She didn't have to be told twice. She took off running in the direction he'd taken. She caught him at the Lawford wagon. Dr. Dorland was there, too.

"We're not interested in eating that poor creature," Martha was telling Tate. "I don't understand how anyone could treat one of God's creatures the way you've done that cow."

Dr. Dorland took up the conversation. "Only a man with absolutely no feeling in his heart could do it. I feel for your family. But about the cow. The meat is infected from her wounds and not fit to eat. I hope no one takes any, Tate, for their sake."

"Well, forget I asked. I shoulda just eaten it all myself." He hiked on down the row of wagons, not stopping at any more.

The next day the Tates stayed to jerk the meat. "We'll still beat you by three days," he told Captain Ransom. "We'll just wait for you and rest."

"I forgot to tell you girls one more thing," Nate said when Rachel returned. "There's another cutoff being built. It won't be finished until fall but it'll cut off one hundred miles and it has more water than the Trail." He sighed. "Won't do us any good, but it'll be a godsend to next year's emigration. It's called Lander's Cutoff."

The next day the train discovered that even on the main trail water was in short supply. They found none all day, not even at their camp. The Butler herd of cows' milk had dwindled from thirty gallons a day to less than one between them all, less than a cup apiece.

The next day, about noon, they reached Green River. The drivers couldn't hold back their parched oxen who pulled the wagons into the river. They camped beside the river so the animals could get their fill of grass and water.

An Indian trading post dominated the spot beside the river. Rachel saw Pastor Richards trade some fishing lures for several pairs of soft white deerskin moccasins.

The three girls and the little boys ran around looking at the colorful flowers.

"Look, Rachel," Willie said. "What are these red things?"

Rachel looked and discovered wild strawberries.

Strawberries! Real strawberries! The girls grabbed pans and picked all they could find.

Petey looked longingly at Martha's pan filled with the red treats. "I wish I was your little boy," he said.

"You can't be my little boy because you already have a mama," Martha said, hugging him, "but you can have half of my berries. Think your mama would like that?"

Petey's brown eyes sparkled with starry sunshine. "Thank you, Martha. I love you."

Rachel gave Martha part of her berries; Martha's family, after all, had more people to feed than her family did. Still, Rachel took home enough of the juicy red fruit for each family member to have a nice dish of them.

It was too cold and windy again for preaching on Sunday, June fourth, so Rachel had a nice day of rest. In the afternoon, the wind died down and Pastor Richards came by her wagon looking as if he'd just stepped from a shower into clean, freshly pressed clothes.

"How about a walk?" he asked.

Rather than hurt him, she tucked up her hair and went. Leading her to all of the train's young women, he invited them to his own wagon.

"What a nice surprise," Tamara said. "I love company."

Pastor Richards got out the moccasins and gave each girl a pair, including Tamara.

"How beautiful," Rachel said, turning hers over and over to see every bead and thread.

"You're welcome," the pastor said. "I wanted you all to have a reason to remember me."

Rachel knew she'd remember Pastor Richards with only friendship in her heart. How could she have thought she felt more?

The next day the oxen started another long hard week.

Rachel, Martha, Julia, Petey, and Willie walked together as always. Rachel hardly noticed when it happened but now she enjoyed the boys and missed them during their nap time.

A bunch of turnarounds told them that five men had been massacred by the Indians a little ways ahead.

"I don't believe them," Martha said. "They're just trying to impress people. And scare them."

Later, they came upon five graves, side-by-side. "Well, so much for what you don't believe," Rachel told Martha. "These are the graves the men told us about."

Finally, they reached the west end of Sublette Cutoff, the road Tate had taken. Not finding Tate waiting for them, they made camp and settled down for the night. That evening, the Tates showed up, wishing they'd stayed with the group.

"We lost two more oxen," Tate said. "And a cow. We can't take our wagon on as we don't have nothin' to pull it."

"I could help you make it into a cart," Nate Butler said. "Maybe your animals could pull it that way."

"No, you aren't," Tate's wife shrilled. "I have to have the things in that wagon."

"Shut up!" Tate said. "I bin listenin' to you too long."

"Then we'll have to keep the half with the cookstove and the dressers." She glared at Nate. "Do you have any idea how much those things cost?" Then she shook her head, answering her own question. "No, I'm sure you wouldn't."

"Ma'am," Nate said, "do you have any idea how much them oxen are worth or where you'll get some more?"

"Make it into a cart," Tate said. "Don't pay no 'tention to her."

It took all that evening and the following day but by the

next day a light, sleek, two-wheeled cart was ready to go. The cookstove and dressers joined the many other items abandoned beside the road.

As the train moved the next morning, Rachel noticed the Tate items. "How can they live with themselves," she said to Martha, "when they killed and tortured several animals by forcing them to haul that stuff up and down the hills. Now it's by the Trail."

Martha shook her dark head. "What a waste of life."

As they walked and talked, Rachel got brave enough to ask Martha what she thought of Pastor Richards.

"I think he's a good man trying to work for God," Martha answered.

But Rachel wasn't satisfied. "I know he's a good man, but I want to know how you feel about him personally. You know what I mean."

Martha smiled her sweet smile. "You mean do I more than like him? Well, I'll tell you the truth. I'm purely not romantically interested in any man, anywhere." She grinned impishly. "He's all yours, Rachel. Or yours, Julia."

"I don't want him," Rachel said. "I may have thought I did once but I know better now. I simply don't want him. He's all yours, Julia."

Julia giggled. "Well, thanks. But what am I going to do with two men? For the whole trip I've liked Dan Barlow a whole lot. But if you don't like the Reverend anymore, Rachel, who is it you do like?"

# eleven

Rachel almost stopped walking as she sucked in her breath. She'd always "liked" someone since she'd been in eighth grade. But who now? She picked up her pace as she thought. "Well," she finally said. "I thought I liked the Reverend just because he's so handsome and tall and clean. Especially clean."

"Did you ever notice how he stays clean?" Julia asked, her eyes twinkling. "He never does a lick of work. Never. Not a lick. I'd rather have a real man."

Rachel laughed. "I told you I discovered I don't care for Pastor Richards that way. But you've put a claim on Dan Barlow so I can't have him."

Julia laughed happily. Obviously they'd finally found a subject entirely to her liking. "I hope you can't," she said giggling, "but I'm not sure. But who do you like now, Rachel?"

Rachel swung her red head back and forth. "There isn't anyone else."

That afternoon while Petey and Willie napped, the Ransom Train caught up with another train, stopped in the Trail. As they walked past the stopped train the girls noticed people standing around in groups. One man stood between two others as if they were restraining him.

The Ransom Train stopped; Martha and Rachel hurried to watch.

"Howdy," Captain Ransom said. "We interruptin' somethin'?"

"We're havin' ourselves a little trial," a white-haired

man said. "Wanna watch?"

"Yes, please," the girls whispered to each other. None had ever seen a trial.

They soon learned that the man had stolen a horse from some Indians, who had probably stolen it from a white man. After he'd been declared guilty, the "judge" told the jury they should determine the man's punishment. About twenty minutes later the jury foreman announced that the man should be "hanged by the neck until dead."

Captain Ransom turned on his heel and rushed back to his own train. "Let's get going," he yelled.

As they walked away, Rachel saw someone hoist the criminal onto the back of a big horse. Someone else climbed into a tree and tied a rope to a low branch, dropping the other end of the rope that was then secured around the man's neck.

"What's going to happen?" Julia asked.

"Someone's going to hit that horse really hard and make him jump out from under the man and he'll be 'hanged until dead,' " George Lawford said.

The girls hurried on looking straight ahead, not caring to see what happened next.

"What if he didn't do it?" Martha asked.

"Better hope he did," Rachel said. " 'Cause he's paying for it anyway."

A few hours later they nooned at Soda Springs, nine or ten sparkling, boiling, bubbling springs of clear water. Someone discovered that by adding a little acid to the water it made a good drink. Rachel and Mama tried it. Not that good, Rachel thought, but something different.

"I'll bet it would be good in biscuits," Mama said. Papa brought a small pail of the water and never had Rachel seen Mama's biscuits rise so high. Mama put the water into jars to take with them.

A fourth of a mile farther they found Steamboat Springs with warm milky water. The train camped there and the women did their washings, the first in hot water since they left Independence. Martha and Rachel did their families' washing, then Mrs. Piling's. The woman hadn't gotten better since Mr. Piling returned from the dead. In fact, as the days passed, she seemed worse.

After the girls finished Mrs. Piling's laundry, they did the wash of several of the horse riders and for Mr. and Mrs. Pitman, an old couple who seemed to be in nearly as bad condition as the oxen. They were considerably older than the fifty-year age limit advised for the vigorous journey, but they'd insisted on coming.

Later that afternoon, as Martha and Rachel returned from doing all the washing, they met Dr. Dorland with a small bloody animal in his hand. Josie's nose twitched as she hurried to Tom.

"I got a gopher for Josie," he said. "Thought she'd be needing another one."

Martha grimaced, then reached for the horrible looking bit of flesh. But Tom drew it back.

"No need for you to touch it," he said. "I'll just give it to Josie." She gladly accepted the bloody morsel, biting it twice before swallowing it whole. Tom laughed and nodded. "I'll keep watching for food for her." He hurried away, wiping his hands on his pants as he went.

The dust continued to plague the travelers and the oxen. Not only did it get into man's and animal's eyes but it piled over the shoe tops making it extremely difficult to walk. Rachel, Martha, Julia, Petey, and Willie wore thin linen handkerchiefs over their eyes and noses.

Rachel noticed the oxen's eyes ran thick with yellowish stuff as they limped along on sore feet. After several failed attempts to help them, she'd learned that she couldn't do anything. But one day Tom Dorland happened by on his mare so she called him over.

"We have to do something for the oxen's eyes," she said. "They're just awful."

His smile faded into a solemn concerned look. "I've noticed," he said. "Not only yours, but all the oxen in the train. It's too hard on them."

"Well, what can we do about it?"

He shook his light head. "The only thing I know would be to stop traveling until the dust dies down. But as far as I can tell, it plans to fly forever."

Disappointment temporarily made Rachel forget she was a brand new Christian and that whatever she said "to the least of these" she said to Jesus.

"Are you going to just let them suffer then? Just say we can't do anything? Not get the train stopped?" Her voice grew louder as she continued. "I thought you cared, Tom Dorland, but you're just like the rest. You're not made of fit material to be a doctor!"

Tom watched her fume for another moment before he grinned. "I'm not an animal doctor," he said softly. "But I do care. I cared about Andy Shackleford, too, but I couldn't help him either." He touched his heels to his horse's sides and trotted off to the front of the line.

One evening they camped by a busy little creek of delightfully cool water where grass grew abundantly. Martha, Julia, and Rachel waded along the creek, enjoying the ice cold water on their feet.

"Look!" Julia shouted, "berries!"

Rachel climbed out of the creek in a hurry and found serviceberries growing thickly on low vines. By that time Martha had pulled herself away from the creek, too, and the girls ran back to the wagons for containers. They filled every pot and pan they could get hold of.

"What'll we do with them?" Martha asked Mrs. Lawford.

Martha's mother was sweet and round, always ready to help the young people. "Well," she said, "we can't take them with us." After thinking a moment, she clapped her hands. "I know. Why don't you make some pies, cobblers, fruit cakes, and whatever you can think up and invite the horse riders to help you eat them?"

So the girls did. Each took some berries and cooked everything she could think of with what she had to cook with. Then Julia ran to invite everyone who wanted to come. Soon, people arrived from all around the wagon circle.

"It smells good," Pastor Richards said with one more exaggerated sniff. "When do we get to eat?"

Stan Latham arrived next with his tin plate and a dirty looking fork. Tom Dorland came next, wearing a wide smile. Dan Barlow came with Tom, both looking as if they anticipated something special. Jackson Lawford trotted into the group, eagerly looking at the treats.

Then Tamara Richards came with her hand through a tall thin man's arm. She looked almost like a real person, Rachel thought. She smiled, her eyes sparkled, and she walked with energy. "I'd like you to meet my friend, Evan Mann," she said almost as if showing off a prize race horse.

"Where'd he come from?" Rachel blurted out. "I thought I'd seen everyone on the train."

"He stays with his wagon and oxen most of the time," Tamara said. She laughed quietly into the man's eyes. "He's shy, but I've been sending him some food, and my brother James shot a few ducks for him, so we got acquainted."

"Good afternoon, Evan Mann," Rachel said, extending her hand. As the man accepted and shook her hand, she recognized him. He was the man who'd tried to catch a rabbit! Rachel tried not to show her recognition and hoped that Martha wouldn't either. It could embarrass the man to be reminded of that hilarious run through the sagebrush.

Julia served Dan first, then herself. They went off somewhere to eat, leaving Rachel and Martha to serve the others. There was plenty of food for everyone who came and several had seconds. Stan Latham alone had thirds.

Pastor Richards led an inspiring collection of songs and preached his usual stirring sermon on June twelfth. Then the group ate lunch together. Rachel felt rather detached since she'd lost interest in the young minister. The silly young men running after the girls meant nothing to her anymore and she wondered how she could have been so enthralled with all of it only a few days ago.

The next morning Rachel happened to be near when the handlers yoked up the oxen for the day's travel. For the first time the oxen tried their best to avoid the yokes. But with a few strong words and two men working together, they forced the heavy yokes onto the oxen's raw necks and shoulders. When the rough wood hit their sores, the animals bawled a moment then quieted as if willing to do what must be done.

Rachel forced back the tears that tried to come into her eyes, then ran around the still-circled wagons to Captain Ransom's wagon.

"Mr. Ransom, you have to stop the wagon train so the oxen can get better," she cried.

The man rose from the box he'd been sitting on. "What's happened, Rachel? Are you all right?"

"No, I'm not. And neither are our oxen. They didn't want the yokes rubbing on their sore necks this morning. They're limping on sore feet and they're getting thinner every day. You have to help me, Captain Ransom."

He shook his thick gray hair. "You're right, girlie. Them oxen need weeks to recuperate. So do some of our people."

Rachel felt a moment's relief but the man continued on.

"Thing is, we don't have time. We're already behind our schedule. Gotta get to Oregon City afore the snow flies. We get caught in the mountains, we'll all die, animals and all." He moved to her, put his arm around her shoulders, and pulled her close. "So we gotta keep movin'. I allays tell the men to treat their animals right, though."

Rachel thanked the man for listening and stumbled back toward her own wagon. At least she knew how it was.

Two days later, just after the wagons corralled, Dan Barlow came to Rachel's wagon. "Miss Lawford," he said quietly, "your father wants you at your wagon right away." Turning his eyes to Julia, he smiled. "See you tonight." Touching his heels to his gelding, he rode ahead.

Martha looked curious. "Strange," she said. "Papa's never called me before. I hope everything's all right. Guess I'd better go find out."

"Want me to come, too?" Rachel asked, staying by Martha's side. "Maybe Julia would watch the boys until we get back."

"I'd love to," Julia said, her eyes still full of stars from her encounter with Dan. "You just go on and do whatever you need to. I'll take good care of them."

When they neared the Lawford wagon, Tom Dorland jumped to the ground and met them a few feet away. "I'm sorry to have to tell you, Miss Lawford, but your mother's sick."

Martha's face lost every semblance of color. "What is it?"

He shook his head. "I can't be sure but it looks bad." He drew in a long breath. "Could be cholera," he murmured.

"No." Martha didn't say more or move a muscle.

But Rachel drew in a long breath and bolted for the wagon, slowing only to jump into it. Mr. Lawford sat on a box near his wife who looked still and small in her feathérbed. Rachel knelt by the woman and took her hand.

"Mrs. Lawford," she said. "I'm here to pray with you."

Mrs. Lawford opened her eyes. "Bless you, dear."

"Oh dear heavenly Father," Rachel began, "we thank You for Your great love for us and giving Your precious only Son to die for us. Oh, Lord, You know how Mrs. Lawford loves You and what a wonderful influence she is on everyone. Please, dear Lord, make her well right away. We all need her so badly. I pray these things in Jesus' precious name, and thank You for hearing and answering my prayer."

Rachel opened her eyes and looked down at Martha's mother, almost expecting to see her get up and start gathering sticks for the supper's fire.

But sweat ran from the woman's unusually red cheeks. She reached a hand to Rachel. "Thank you dear, for that lovely prayer. I'm sure He'll have me up in a day or so."

Rachel, on her knees, leaned down and kissed the hot cheek. "Of course He will," she whispered. "Now you sleep for a while and don't worry. We'll take good care of Willie."

"I know," the sick woman said, her eyelashes falling against her cheeks.

Rachel jumped to the ground where Martha and Tom still talked. Tom smiled at her. "Got yourself all exposed, did you?"

Rachel hadn't given that possibility a thought. Well, if

there was anything to be exposed to, she probably did. "I might have," she admitted.

"I'll be back in a couple of hours," he told Martha.

Martha didn't talk much. "We'll keep Willie tonight," Rachel said. "And I'll come over later to see what Tom says."

On being told that his mama was sick, Willie agreed to stay with Rachel. After the supper things were cleaned up and put away, Rachel hurried to the Lawford wagon. Martha met her outside and told her Tom was certain her mama had cholera.

"I'm going to help take care of her and make her well," Rachel said. "I'll be over in the morning."

The next morning Captain Ransom called a day's stop for the train to give Mrs. Lawford a chance to recover.

The woman had worsened during the night, Rachel learned when she arrived at Martha's wagon. "You go do something or rest," she told her dear friend.

Mr. Lawford sat on his wooden box in the wagon, looking heartbroken. "Don't you worry, Mr. Lawford," Rachel said. "We'll have her on her feet in no time. You just sit here and watch and listen if you want."

First she wet washrags in cold water and put them on Mrs. Lawford's hot forehead.

"That feels so good," the woman whispered. "Please, don't stop."

"I won't," she told the weak woman. "I'm going to be here and keep them on you all day."

She applied the cold compresses and read the Gospel of John to the Lawfords most of the day. Both listened quietly to every word. But, every time she stopped to cool the washrag, Mr. Lawford asked how his wife was now.

Tom came by a little later. "I don't know if you're helping her physically, but you're doing them both a world of good," he told Rachel. "As you read, you're giving them something positive to think about and the wet cloths certainly do make her feel better." He smiled a gentle smile. "Since you already got yourself exposed, I'll just say keep up the good work."

At noon Rachel stopped and made some rabbit broth from a rabbit Jackson Lawford had brought and cleaned. After giving Mr. Lawford a bowl and spooning some into Mrs. Lawford's mouth, she went back to her reading and applying the cold compresses.

"What have you been doing today?" Rachel asked when Martha finally appeared at the wagon.

"I've been doing people's washing," she said. "I had a feeling I'd be busy when washing day came so I got it done today. How's my mama?"

"I don't know," Rachel said. "She's not talking as much as she was this morning."

Rachel ran back to her own wagon just in time for supper. Willie and Julia had gathered sticks for the fire and Mama had biscuits and side meat cooking.

Willie slept in Rachel's wagon again and morning came quickly. After breakfast, Rachel hurried to the Lawford wagon again. Martha ran to meet her.

"Papa's sick, too," Martha whispered. "They're both awfully sick."

Both girls worked all day caring for Martha's parents. Both seemed too sick to listen to reading but Rachel did it anyway, just in case. Rachel cared mostly for Mrs. Lawford and Martha took care of her father. At noon, both girls fixed broth for Martha's parents.

"Papa thinks I'm Mama," Martha whispered. "Oh, Rachel, I'm afraid they aren't going to get well."

"Yes, they are," Rachel snapped. "God will make them well."

# twelve

Tom Dorland came by several times that day and left looking sadder each time. One time Rachel found him kneeling beside Mrs. Lawford, his hand on her forehead, praying earnestly for her and Mr. Lawford.

That night Rachel stayed with Martha to help. Mrs. Lawford died early in the morning. Mr. Lawford didn't know. He died that afternoon.

Pastor Richards said a few words, prayed for Martha, Jackson, and Willie, then they buried Mr. and Mrs. Lawford in the Trail. The emigrants yoked up to continue on and many wagons ran over the graves, trying to hide them from Indians and animals. And the wagon train moved forward. Always forward. Relentlessly forward.

Jackson guided the Lawford oxen who seemed nearly as broken as he. They could hardly walk and Jackson could barely hold his head erect.

Martha, Rachel, Julia, Petey, and Willie walked with Jackson. Rachel thought she couldn't bear losing the Lawfords. They had been good to her, even when she hadn't been all that nice to anyone.

"Why didn't God heal them?" she kept asking Martha. "We prayed so hard. Even Tom prayed."

"We can't understand everything," Martha said, "but just keep on trusting Him, Rachel. He knows the beginning from the end."

Those words didn't satisfy Rachel. "What's the use praying if He doesn't answer?" she asked bitterly.

Martha remained calm. "I'm not sure. Maybe we'll go

through some horrible hardships that would have been harder for them than to die quickly and peacefully. This may have been the best way. No, I said that wrong. This was the best way. God loved them much more than we did, and He wanted the best for them even more than we did. But He knows all. And don't forget that death isn't the end, Rachel. There's a beautiful home in a beautiful world waiting for them. . .and for us. Please don't lose your faith."

As the days passed, Rachel thought about the things Martha had said. Finally, they made sense to her. She felt better and God's sweet peace returned to her heart.

One day they neared Fort Hall, 1300 miles from Independence. Abandoned wagons, household goods, and dead animals grew thicker around them. As they drew close to the large fort, Jackson called Martha to him. Rachel moved closer, too, as they walked along the dusty trail.

"Have you noticed the oxen can barely walk?" he asked.

Martha nodded. "I've noticed, Jackson. It's really sad, but what can we do?"

He gave her a long look. "They're giving out, Martha. See them stumbling? Almost blindly? They're going to die within two days. We'll have to leave them at Fort Hall. With rest and some good food they might recover. Otherwise, they're dead."

"Leave them, Martha," Rachel cried. "Give them a chance to live."

"But what will we do?" Martha asked. "We don't have extra oxen like you."

"Martha!" Jackson said. "Either we leave them and hope for the best or they're dead. They can't help us if they're dead."

"Leave them," Rachel repeated. "We have extra oxen. I'll get Papa to put some on your wagon."

So that's what they did. The fresh oxen pulled with a strength that the Lawford animals hadn't had for weeks.

The next day after they left the oxen, Jackson called Martha to him again as they walked. "I keep thinking I need to go back on the Trail and meet Aunt Mandy and Uncle Cleve," he said. "They deserve to know what happened."

"No, Jackson," Martha pleaded. "You have to care for the oxen while I watch Willie."

He walked a while then continued. "I have to, don't you see? I just have to, Martha. Someone will help you with the oxen."

Martha begged and pleaded with Jackson but couldn't change his mind.

The next morning he gathered his clothes, a little food, and climbed onto his horse. "As soon as I tell them what happened I'll come right back," he said. "I won't be gone more than a few days, so wish me well."

"I'll try," Martha said in a small voice. "But you shouldn't be doing this. The oxen are your responsibility."

"I'll tell you what I think," Rachel said. "I think you're not even a man but a big baby. Don't you think Martha hurts as much as you? And poor little Willie. How's he going to feel when you run off?"

"Sorry," Jackson mumbled. "It's something I have to do." He touched his horse's sides with his heels and took off trotting, back the way they'd come.

On Sunday, June nineteenth, the warm sunny weather lifted Rachel's spirits. And she hadn't heard a single mosquito during the night! Could it be that they were through with that plague?

Pastor Richards preached a stirring sermon on having

faith when it seems all reason for faith is gone. "Faith isn't faith," he said, "when all goes well. Faith is believing when all looks dark and your prayers don't seem to be heard. That's real faith. And our Lord will help you with this faith if you only ask."

The people shared the noon meal so they could all be together on their day of rest.

As Martha, Willie, Rachel, and Julia filled their plates, Pastor Richards approached, this time giving Rachel his attention.

"Would you lovely young ladies mind if a tired old preacher joined you for dinner?" he asked.

Before Rachel had a chance to panic, Stan Latham crowded between Pastor Richards and her.

"You look uncommonly lovely today, Miss Butler," he said in his oily smooth voice. "I'd like the privilege of sharing the meal with you."

Suddenly, she looked longingly at Pastor Richards. At least she could eat with him sitting there. She'd almost for sure throw up if the filthy Stan Latham were in sight. What could she do?

Before she answered, another oh-so-welcome voice broke the stillness—Tom Dorland.

"Oh, Miss Butler, there you are," Tom said. "I need your help right away. . .if you have time. I need to medicate a couple of bad eyes and can't do it alone."

Rachel jumped to her feet before Tom finished. "I'm ready," she said, heaving a huge sigh of relief. "Let's go."

As they walked away from the dinner, Rachel felt a stab of remorse for having left Martha at the mercy of Stan Latham. "Where is this person who needs treatment?" she asked.

Tom grinned. His eyes had a lovely glow that Rachel

hadn't seen before. Come to think of it she may have never noticed his eyes at all. The soft look must come from his close relationship with God. "Did I say it was a person?" he asked. "I had in mind treating your oxen's eyes with some boric acid. It might make them feel better."

Rachel stopped in her tracks. "What's going on, Dr. Dorland? I tried hard to get you to help those oxen and you refused. What's changed?"

They reached Rachel's wagon where Tom had stashed the medicine. "Well, I mixed up this stuff and decided to try it," he said. "If you still want to, that is." Then they took the medicine and went searching for the oxen but couldn't find them.

"They're somewhere gorging on grass," Rachel said. "Wouldn't it be better to do it while they're yoked?"

He nodded. "I think you're right." He grinned mischievously again. "So, should we go get something to eat?"

Rachel laughed and headed back toward the dinner. "Well, I'm glad you thought about the oxen and got me away from Stan Latham. I panicked when that pig showed up."

"Oh, one more thing," Tom said as they neared the crowd of people. "When we finish eating, I have to take some food to the Pitmans. If you help me, we can do it in one trip."

As they reached the rest of the people, Rachel agreed to help. Pastor Richards and Stan Latham still sat with Martha and Julia. Dan Barlow was there, too, sitting close to Julia. Tom and Rachel filled their plates and joined them. Rachel faced away from Stan Latham and pretended he wasn't there.

Later, Rachel and Tom carried a nice meal to the

Pitmans who thanked them profusely. As they walked back to Rachel's wagon, she thought about the old couple.

"Will the Pitmans get cholera and die?"

He shook his head. "We can hope and pray they won't."

When they reached Rachel's wagon, Tom seemed reluctant to leave. They talked a little about Martha, how brave she was, left all alone with Willie, the wagon, and the oxen.

The next day they traveled on. Soon, the sun became scorching.

"The dust comes over my shoes," Willie complained, "and it hurts."

"I know," Martha told him tenderly. "It comes over mine, too. Try to put your feet straight down when you step."

He couldn't so Martha carried him a while. "It's hot on my feet, too," she told the little boy. "Can you walk now?"

He walked a while then she carried him again, all the time keeping the oxen going. Petey managed to keep going on his own.

Early in the afternoon they came to Fall River which they had to ford. The deep river with steep banks looked impassible.

"How can we go across that?" Petey asked.

"I don't know," Martha said. "Shall we sit here and watch?"

Soon, they saw the men putting secure ropes around a wagon, then tying the ropes to five yoke of oxen. With men guiding both the wagon and the oxen, they let the wagon down the steep cliff. They lowered all the wagons the same way.

Then the same weary oxen pulled the wagons across the deep swift stream. The men made it as safe as possible by hooking several wagons together and doing the same with the oxen. At near dusk, the last wagon emerged from the river and Captain Ransom called corralling time.

The next morning the road turned into a big rock pile. Big rocks, little rocks, smooth rocks, sharp rocks. So many rocks that when the oxen stepped onto one it rolled onto the others, causing the weary animals to stumble and nearly fall. The girls had the same problem.

The sun beat down so hot that Rachel saw little heat waves coming off the oxen and felt herself wavering, too. She couldn't see one bush or even sagebrush anywhere to shade people or animals from the burning sun. They nooned at a place where they found a little patch of grass but it wasn't nearly large enough to satisfy the famished animals.

"Why did you stop here?" Rachel yelled at Captain Ransom. "Can't you see the animals need more food?"

"I've heard about enough out of you, young lady!" Ransom shouted back. "Just where am I supposed to find grass, anyway?"

"There must be some if you'd just look harder," Rachel yelled, then burst into tears. Why did she act so mean, anyway? Ransom had never been unkind before. She voiced her worries to Martha.

"He's doing his best," Martha said. "It's the heat that's causing people to lose control. Just ask God to help you be kind."

While Rachel and her mother fixed dinner, Rachel heard people yelling at each other from other wagons and decided Martha was right. The heat made people crazy.

Just before dinner was ready, Papa left the area and Mama asked Rachel to find him. She ran all over looking for him, finally finding him with Captain Ransom.

"I've been looking all over for you," she said much

louder than necessary. "Why do you run off just when dinner's ready?"

"I'm not your child," he yelled. "I'll go where I want whenever I want if it's all the same with you."

Rachel wheeled around to run back to the wagon and ran into Tom Dorland. "Why do you have to sneak up on me all the time?" she yelled at him. "You could at least let a person know you're coming."

He opened his mouth, closed it and remained silent a moment. "I'm sorry," he finally said. "I didn't intend to sneak up on you." His voice remained sweet and calm.

Embarrassed at being so unkind, Rachel turned her back on him and tore back to her wagon where she realized she wasn't representing God very well. No, she wasn't representing Him at all. "Please forgive me, Father," she whispered. "I'm sorry to be so terrible. I hope You won't give up on me." Immediately, she had a strong feeling that she should ask Captain Ransom, Tom Dorland, and Papa to forgive her. But she was much too hot to find all of them right now.

Each day was the same. Scorching heat, burning dust, and people yelling at each other. All except Tom and Martha. Those two stayed nice no matter what.

On June twenty-sixth, every creature needed the rest so badly and the sun stayed so hot that many didn't turn out for Pastor Richards's service or the potluck dinner afterward. Rachel attended though, so Martha wouldn't be alone. They didn't even have their plates filled when Pastor Richards joined them. Speaking especially to Rachel, he talked about his sermon, the singing, his hard-to-keep-pressed clothing, and his absent parishioners.

She tried to listen patiently, wondering how she'd ever thought he might be the man for her. About the time they finished eating, Tom, who hadn't eaten with the group, arrived with another small dead animal for Josie.

The next morning the train started early and traveled hard. Rachel thought her feet would burn up, even through her shoes. The dust on the ground burned so hot she couldn't keep her hand on it. Finally, after what seemed like forever, the train stopped to camp at Salmon Falls. Tepees, ponies, and Indians swarmed everywhere. One Indian brought a thirty-five-pound salmon to swap for old clothes. Several families traded clothes for the Indian's huge fish.

The Indian gave the fish to Papa, then looked the clothes over. He seemed pleased until he found a long rip in one shirt. With hand motions he requested a needle and thread that someone provided. Then, he sat on his heels and went to work on the tear. A few minutes later, he handed the needle back, nodding and wearing a wide smile. Rachel signed for him to hold up the shirt for her to see. Surprised, she discovered the Indian had used some skill in repairing the shirt.

The next day as they traveled, carcasses became so thick they almost blocked the Trail. The overpowering stench seemed more than the emigrants could bear. And graves became so numerous Rachel lost count.

When they stopped that evening, one of Thurman Tate's oxen dropped dead in the yoke. The other's legs gave way and it couldn't get up. The next morning the ox still couldn't get up so Tate had to leave it there. He also had to leave the cart. Several families took a few of the Tates' clothes but all their oxen were too worn-out to carry much more so the rest of the Tates' belongings were left alongside the Trail.

"I wish someone would tell that man how much misery and death his greediness has caused innocent animals,"

Rachel groused.

The train continued on all day with no grass or water for the oxen. At five o'clock that afternoon they reached the river and, in their eagerness for water, the oxen pulled the wagons into the river again.

So desperately did the animals need the nourishment that the guides went off the Trail, looking for grass. The train was stopped any time someone found grass.

The next day the train came to a good camp at Glenn's Ferry at Three Island Crossing, 1398 miles from home. As the people prepared for the Sabbath and Rachel and Martha washed clothes, Rachel told Martha they'd never see civilization again.

On Sunday, July third, people came from all around to hear the preaching and share the meal. Since no one had much food anymore, the potlucks consisted mostly of beans, biscuits, and dried apple pie. Fewer and fewer people came to the dinners.

The next morning everyone repacked and threw away anything they could live without. They'd done this so many times that Rachel wondered how there could be anything left. But more items edged the road each time. When everyone was ready, the people lined up to be ferried across the river. All except Mark Piling.

"I ain't makin' those cutthroats rich," he said. "I'll just get myself across and save the money."

"Better not," Nate Butler said. "They say the river's ruthless here."

"Who says?" Piling asked scornfully. "The men who run the ferry?"

Rachel, Martha, Julia, Petey, and Willie sat on the river bank to watch Piling ford the river.

But Mr. Piling came after Petey. "You get yourself over

to our wagon!" he bellowed at the trembling little boy. "Fergot you even had a family din't you?" As Petey skittered past his father, Piling reached out a hand and cuffed the back of Petey's head, knocking him, face first, into the dust. "Get up!" Piling yelled. "Get into that wagon and make sure the water don't get too high." Petey scrambled to his feet, tears running down his dirty face, and raced ahead of Mr. Piling to the wagon.

Piling hooked his oxen to the wagon and started them into the river. The animals balked several times and Piling rewarded them with hard lashes from the whip. Eventually, they made it to the first island. Then, with more lashing, the oxen reached the second island. They'd nearly made it across.

"It's going to be all right now," Julia breathed.

But, just as she spoke, a swift undercurrent snatched the wagon, tipping it over. Mr. Piling, who'd been in the river with the oxen, grabbed his wife as she tumbled from the wagon. Mrs. Piling held tightly to the baby but Petey whirled past them and on down the river.

# thirteen

Martha screamed and bolted toward the river. Rachel caught her just in time to stop her from plunging in after Petey. Mr. Piling held on tight to his wife and baby, watching Petey spin and whirl down the river until he disappeared from sight.

A moment later, the oxen became tangled in the harness and cumbersome yoke and couldn't keep their heads above the water. One of them managed to let out a loud bawl as they careened down the river, over and under the wagon. Soon,the wagon's contents littered the surface of the river and parts of the wagon bounced on the water until they lined the far bank.

"Go get him!" Martha screamed to anyone who might be listening. "Go get Petey! He's in the river!"

No one plunged into the river, but many people ran down the banks looking for the little boy.

Rachel had to restrain Martha again. As Martha screamed and struggled, Rachel thanked God she was bigger and stronger than Martha. Rachel had never seen Martha upset before, let alone in a horrible state like this.

"You can't go into the river hoping to find Petey," Rachel said quietly. "You'd only drown yourself." Martha continued to struggle with all her strength. "Martha," Rachel said a little louder, "you have Willie to care for. Remember, Martha?"

Finally, Martha wilted in Rachel's arms, her strength gone. "They aren't going to save him," she murmured over and over and over. Finally, she quieted.

The men looked for Petey all that night and until noon the next day. Early in the afternoon Pastor Richards held a short service for Petey after which wagon train moved on.

The Rahns took in Mr. and Mrs. Piling and the baby. The Pilings had nothing left for anyone to haul. Rachel walked to a spot where she could see Mrs. Piling. She looked like a snow white dead person with no expression at all.

The train traveled five miles to a good camp at Wickahoney Creek. Rachel stayed with Martha that night. Poor confused Willie stayed with Rachel's parents. Martha, who had been so brave when her parents died, went completely to pieces now. She cried and moaned all night; in the rare moments she slept, she called out for the little boy. Rachel cradled her in her arms and held her tightly.

Pastor Richards came to Martha but she turned him away. "Rachel's taking care of me," she said. "I don't need anyone else. No one cares anyway, not even God."

Rachel, realizing their roles had been reversed, reminded Martha that God loved Petey even more than they did and that He was crying with them. "Petey'll wake up with Jesus in the most beautiful home he's ever had," she promised. "Jesus will love him and never hurt him. Mark Piling hurt Petey, Martha. Haven't you noticed how Petey kept away from his father? And how he hurt him that last day? Maybe God took Petey away from his father to protect him from more pain and suffering."

After several days of crying and listening to Rachel explain how God let this happen to save Petey from his abusive father, Martha seemed to accept Petey's death. She clung to Willie and didn't mention Petey anymore, though her white face told of her continued suffering.

"I want you to remember one thing," Rachel told Martha as they trudged along beside the oxen one day. "You gave Petey more happiness than he'd ever known. I know you did. And you taught him to love Jesus. Day after day you taught him of Jesus' love for him. That's something for you to rejoice about. We both know how much Petey loved Jesus, don't we?"

Martha smiled tremulously and nodded. "We purely do. Thank you, Rachel for being so good for me right now. You've become a real Christian."

But, inside, Rachel wasn't sure about that. She felt so furious with Piling she thought she couldn't handle having him around anymore. One day she told Martha how she felt about the man. "I wish he'd died instead of Petey!" she said. "Mrs. Piling would have been glad, too. I know she would."

Martha took her eyes from the oxen and hugged Rachel. "I know how you feel," she said. "But we can't feel that way. Remember the Lord's Prayer says God will forgive us as we forgive others. Let's ask God to help us forgive Mr. Piling. Let's pray for God to touch Mr. Piling's heart, too." So the girls prayed right then and there.

Still, Rachel couldn't stop thinking about Mr. Piling, and her thoughts weren't good.

One day Captain Ransom stopped the train when a little girl, Jennie, fell in front of a wagon and an ox walked on her. Tom Dorland sent someone after Rachel to help him.

"You have to hold her still while I pull her leg into place," he said in his kind but firm voice.

Rachel held the child, murmuring encouragement into her ear, doubting the girl heard over all her screaming.

"There," Tom said a while later. And, in the middle of a sob, the little girl stopped crying. Rachel looked up with a question in her eyes. Tom smiled. "The bone snapped into place," he explained. "I'm sorry I had to hurt you," he told the little girl. "I won't hurt you any-more." Then he instructed Rachel how to help him put the splint on the leg in the most comfortable way. An hour later they finished and Rachel felt as if she'd been running all day.

"You're the best helper I've ever had," Tom said, his eyes showing his appreciation. "You really must consider going into medicine."

Rachel laughed quietly. "I'll do that," she said. "I'll enter the first medical school I find in Oregon City." Then she thought of Piling. "May I talk to you a minute?" she asked.

"Sure. I'll carry Jennie back to her parents first. Then we can walk for a little while."

When they finally stood where no one could hear them, Rachel felt shy to be talking to Tom like this. He was so good, he probably never had a negative thought about anyone. But she'd brought him here and she would share her thoughts. "I can't stop thinking about Mr. Piling," she said softly. "I can't stand the man, Tom, and I don't think he should be allowed to stay on the train. Could you ask the captain to put him off?"

Tom looked surprised for just a second then cleared his face of expression. "I wonder if you've thought this through," he finally said. "If Ransom puts Piling off the train, his wife and baby will go, too. And those poor people have had it rough enough already, don't you think?"

True enough, Rachel hadn't intended for the wife and baby to go, but they probably would.

Tom smiled kindly at Rachel. "I understand how you feel and I suspect most of the people on the train feel the same way. But we're a Christian group, remember?"

A few days later they met four more turnarounds. "You oughta go back while you can," they said. "It's nothin' but desert fer a long ways. By then it'll be winter and you'll never git through the Blues. Them mountains is killers. They kill the oxen and people just the same."

The men from the Ransom Train huddled around the four trying to decide how much the men knew and how much they surmised. "We must be almost through the desert," Dan Barlow said. "The Mormon guidebook says—"

Suddenly, one of the turnarounds pointed a finger at Dan. "I know you," he yelled. Then he turned to the others. "You'uns know who you got on this here train? That cur's a horse thief. I seen him escape just before he got hisself hanged. 'Twas in Illinois, it was. Ran right through the crowd, grabbed the sheriff's own horse, and escaped. In broad daylight, he did. Get a rope, boys. Let's finish the job."

"Just hold on here," Captain Ransom said quietly. "This here's my son and he's been with me all his life. Never set foot in no state but Missouri. Musta been someone else. Come on, let's get this thing movin'."

"Hey," the accuser yelled, "I know that face for sure. He's the man. Get him, boys. 'Tain't right for a man to flout the law." The other three men converged on Dan who made no effort to protect himself.

Stan Latham turned to Tom Dorland and Nate Butler. "Grab your guns," Stan said. Almost instantly, a dozen men had guns, all aimed at the turnarounds.

"Turn the man loose," Nate demanded. "We don't want a war over this but you can't come in here and abduct the captain's son."

The turnarounds released Dan, backed to their horses, mounted, and galloped away, cursing loudly.

After the men were nearly out of sight, Dan turned to Ransom. "I'm the man, Captain. I stole a horse when I was nineteen, old enough to know better. I thank you all for defending me but I'm ready to pay for my crime now."

Captain Ransom shook his wiry gray hair. "The Dan Barlow on this train always pulls his weight and then some. He's had plenty of opportunities to help himself to things but never has. He's allays thinking of the other guy. No, the Dan Barlow on this train isn't a taker, but a giver." He looked around at the circle of men then back to Dan. "The Dan Barlow on this train is a genyooine born again Christian and I don't want to hear you or no one else say or even think anything foul about this here Dan. Is that clear?" No one said a word, but some flickering smiles met Ransom's stern command.

The train started to move again and, as always, Rachel and Julia walked with Martha and her borrowed oxen, helping her as they could and especially entertaining Willie, who kept asking for Petey.

"Wasn't that exciting?" Julia asked, referring to the encounter with the turnarounds.

"A little too exciting," Rachel said. "Someone could have gotten hurt."

"But isn't Dan brave? And isn't the captain wonderful? Imagine him, claiming Dan for his son."

"That was because he knows Dan's a really sincere Christian now," Martha said, "a new person in Christ. He'd never have done that if Dan was the same man who stole the horse."

"Have you decided to go on to Oregon City?" Rachel asked Martha for the millionth time.

"I purely can't," Martha said. "Jackson and my aunt and uncle and cousin will come looking for Willie and me there. And Josie, of course."

"Jackson doesn't deserve to find you," Rachel snapped. "He should spend the rest of his life looking for you." She pointed at the oxen and the wagon, then down at Willie. "Look what he left."

Martha nodded. "He shouldn't have done that. Sometimes I still get mad at him for it, but he's kin, Rachel. So are my aunt and uncle. They're all Willie and I have left."

"You have me. And I love you more than all of them put together."

Martha smiled but shook her head. "I love you, too. I'd rather go on with you, Rachel. I purely would. But I have to stop. I have to."

Later that afternoon the Trail ran so close to a ten-foot embankment beside the river there was barely room for the oxen driver to walk beside the animals.

Tom Dorland appeared on foot. "You'd better let me take the oxen for a while" he said to Martha. "If they balk just a little they'll push you right off the cliff into the river."

"These oxen are just like Josie," Martha said. "They wouldn't hurt me for anything."

Tom reached for the small walking stick Martha carried. He grinned. "Where's your whip?"

She smiled back at him. "I don't need a whip with these nice boys. Once in a while I guide them a little with the stick, but I haven't had to hurt them even once."

"Okay, I'll use the stick for a cane, all right?"

Martha heaved a sigh of relief as she fell back with Rachel, Julia, and Willie, behind the wagon. She started singing Jesus songs with Willie right away, and the girls joined in. After a while Rachel noticed a strong, clear tenor harmonizing with them—Tom.

Tom walked with the oxen until stopping time that

afternoon, then unyoked them and took them off to pasture.

Martha and Willie stayed with their wagon to eat their meal and Rachel ran back to hers where she found Mama trying to get some sagebrush to burn.

"The trouble is," Mama said, puffing from her efforts, "when it catches, it burns so quickly it puts out hardly any heat."

Between Mama and Rachel they finally got the fire going and made biscuits. By now their supplies were low, the cows had long since given up trying to make milk, so the meals grew simpler and simpler. Every now and then Papa shot a bird or rabbit and that made a big difference. The biscuits were only flour, baking powder, salt, and water. They had side meat with them and sometimes beans, but not tonight. They felt lucky to get enough heat to cook the biscuits and side meat.

"When we reach a trading post, we'll replenish our supplies," Papa said. "That shouldn't be too long."

It was even a shorter time than Papa thought. They camped about where the Owyhee River joins the Snake, three miles from Fort Boise.

On July tenth, Sunday, the group had their usual singing meeting and preaching but so many Indians, trappers, soldiers, and emigrants, came and went that it didn't feel very restful to Rachel.

The next day, about midmorning, the train reached Fort Boise. The fort was a small replica of Fort Hall, made from adobe bricks like all the other forts, but was much smaller. They traveled along the Snake River where a few patches of grass grew. The train still stopped for the grass but thankfully it wasn't quite so rare anymore. They'd seen no trees or even shrubs between Fort Hall and Fort Boise, but at least now they seemed to be through the desert.

Rachel's father bought much-needed supplies at the fort, as did others who still had money left.

As a group walked away from the fort, a whiskered old man told them to be careful about drinking cold water. "Lots of people have died from exactly that," he said.

After they'd gotten away from the man, Tom leaned toward Rachel. "I think that man is miles off. The only time we shouldn't drink water is when it's contaminated. The Good Lord gave us water for cleansing the body, inside and out, and history will prove me right."

Rachel believed him. Come to think of it, she'd probably believe anything he said.

"Let me take the oxen a while," Rachel said one day to Martha who never complained about being tired, or anything else.

"I can do it," Martha said. "They're so good it isn't very hard."

"Get out of my way," Rachel said in play. "They're my oxen and I'll lead them part time." After that Rachel led the oxen half of each day. Julia watched Willie part of the time, and Tom and Dan took a turn with the oxen several times a week.

One day they stayed in camp until two o'clock to let the cattle feed. That day they left the Snake River for the last time and before the day ended, reached Burnt River where they expected to have plenty of water and grass for the animals. They seemed to be out of the desert.

July twenty-fourth, Sunday, the train enjoyed a good rest without throngs of people running around and through their camp. Rachel truly enjoyed the uninterrupted singing and sermon that day. The minister talked again about

God's unfathomable love for us. How He loves each of us much much more than we love our children.

Rachel carried the message in her heart and felt better every time she thought about it.

The group put their food together even though it was a pitiful thing to call a potluck. Martha though, didn't come, so Rachel went looking for her.

"I couldn't come," Martha explained. "All we have to eat is Trail Bread, without most of the things that make it Trail Bread." She laughed. "It's just flour, salt, and water. But Willie eats it and so does Josie."

"Well, you come anyway," Rachel said. "I'll get Mama to fry some extra side meat for you to bring."

As the meal began, Stan Latham showed up and asked Julia Tate if he could join her for the meal. When Rachel saw the cornered look in the younger girl's eyes she thought she might grab Julia's hand and run anywhere. But Tom Dorland happened by and told Latham his horses were leaving the area. Latham hurried off to check his animals, Tom beside him.

Pastor Richards asked Rachel if he could eat with her. Rachel said of course, and called Martha to join them. Julia ate with them, too.

Later that afternoon Tom showed up and asked Rachel to help him. "I need to check Sandra Piling," he explained. "She's failed a lot on the trip."

After checking the woman over, Tom talked to Mr. Piling. "She seems to be failing quickly. You'd better keep her in bed and feed her the best food you can beg, borrow, or shoot."

"Who's gonna fix all that wonderful food if Sandra's in bed?" Mr. Piling asked.

# fourteen

A look of surprise flitted across Tom's face then disappeared. "I thought you'd cook for your family," he said, "but if you can't or don't have time, I'd be glad to do it for you."

Rachel almost laughed when Tom offered to cook. But Mr. Piling didn't. "Ain't got 'nough food for you," he groused.

"Oh, I'll eat before I come," Tom said. "I won't eat your food."

Piling didn't say any more so Tom and Rachel headed back to Rachel's wagon. When they got there she turned to thank him for walking her home, and caught a strange but gentle look in his eyes.

"So," he said with a chuckle, "I caught you laughing at the thought of my cooking, didn't I?"

"I hope not," she said with a giggle of her own.

"Well, I did, and I'll have you know I can cook anything. . .as long as it's boiled potatoes. Alas, I haven't seen a potato for months."

The next morning the wagons creaked as tired oxen plodded along with sore feet and necks, almost too weak to pull the wagons. Rachel watched Martha gently urge her animals along, while hearing the sound of whips and anguished bawls, together with rough male voices yelling at their oxen. She told herself that Martha probably got more out of her animals than the cruel men did.

Vultures blackened the carcasses on and beside the Trail. As the wagon train passed, the huge birds rose into the air screaming their displeasure at having their meals interrupted, then waited impatiently nearby until the train passed and they could continue their feast.

Late in the afternoon the train came upon a man with a baby in his left arm. The other arm hung bloody and useless; blood covered his clothes, too.

"Dorland!" Captain Ransom yelled, stopping the train. "What's going on?" he asked the man.

"Well, sir, my wife died about a week ago. Two days later, two of my oxen died and the others couldn't pull the wagon, so I left them. I took my horse and four mules and started out but before long, Indians attacked and took the animals." The man grimaced. "They like horses and mules a lot better then oxen. I'm thankin' the good Lord they didn't hurt the baby."

Tom appeared about then, looking to Rachel like the most beautiful person in the entire world. The man who helped everyone. He glanced through the faces until he found her. "I'll need you," he said softly.

After Mama took the baby, Rachel helped Tom clean the man's wounds with whiskey. The brave man stiffened but didn't utter a sound. Then, she held the man's arm as Tom stitched the wound. When he finished, he looked at Rachel. "Seventy-five stitches," he said smiling. "Looks pretty neat, doesn't it?" Then she helped him put the man's arm in a sling.

The thought passed through Rachel's mind that whoever married Tom Dorland would have to share him with the world. How awful!

Then she realized his compassion had a lot to do with why she loved him. She loved Tom? Yes! She loved him! She loved Dr. Tom Dorland! All she could ever want would be to help him help the world. . .all the time . . .forever. No doubt about it, she loved this man she'd been helping all along the Trail. But, suddenly she felt shy, as if she had to get away from him.

"Are we through now?" she asked quietly.

"Yes, for now. Thanks, Rachel. You're always a big help."

"The man and his baby will be sleeping in your wagon," Papa told her when they stopped that night. "There was no other place for them. You can sleep in ours."

Rachel surprised herself and her father by not minding. She'd be just fine with her parents.

The next morning they passed through miles and miles of prairie where the grass had been burned off, leaving a black stinking mess.

"That's the Indians' way of stopping the white man," Julia said. "Dan told me the Indians are trying to starve our cattle so we'll go back where we came from."

"I wonder how far it goes," Martha said. "We thought our animals would have plenty to eat now." But the cattle went all day without grass.

That night they camped by Powder River with plenty of grass and water. As the girls inspected their campsite, they discovered the river was alive with salmon.

When they spread the news, many men brought their guns to shoot some fish for supper, a dream come true for the weary travelers. The men all tried but no one could hit the fish. Finally, Tom looked up at the watching girls and flashed a smile. Rachel's heart melted into a small puddle in her chest. But he didn't give her any special looks or seem to notice.

"I'm going to shoot under the fish," he called. "We'll see what happens." He hit the fish, pulled it out, and the men crowded around. "Just shoot a few inches under the fish," he said. The men thinned out one by one, as they each shot a couple of the large creatures and hauled them off toward home.

To go with the fish, Mama made biscuits that she'd wrapped in clay and buried in the coals. Rachel invited

Martha and Willie to enjoy the feast with them.

After they finished, Rachel took half of a fish to Tom to share with the Pilings. Trembling at the thought of meeting him, Rachel nearly turned back, but forced herself on. The Piling's needed the food.

Tom's welcoming smile showed no change. He couldn't tell that she loved him. She'd thought a sign, RACHEL'S IN LOVE WITH TOM, might be emblazoned on her forehead.

As they delivered the large piece of fish to the Pilings, all Rachel could think about was her love for Tom. Tom, who stood about five feet, nine inches tall, was slim, blond, and boyish looking and was exactly opposite from the dream man she'd carried in her mind all these years. Oh, but he was exactly her dream. She forced the personal thoughts from her mind so she could be casual with him. Mark Piling didn't even thank them for the food but Sandra did.

As they walked back to the Butler wagon, Tom told Rachel to tell Martha to thoroughly cook some salmon and feed it to Josie. Rachel cooked a large fish and took half of it to Josie, who wolfed it down as if it were half a slice of bread, her tail thrashing the air wildly. When Josie finished, she leaned against Rachel and gave her hand a few sloppy kisses. "I love you, too, Josie," Rachel whispered to the shaggy dog.

Rachel took the other half of the big fish to the Pitmans, the older couple who were doing better now. Through tears, they thanked Rachel for her thoughtfulness. Rachel walked away completely happy. Martha was right. . .nothing satisfied more than helping other people and dogs.

Back at the wagon, she stopped to relax and she realized how cold the evening had become. What a change from the burning heat they'd endured for the last few weeks.

The next day the girls found themselves walking on

rock piles again. Rocks on rocks on rocks. The oxen struggled valiantly to pull the wagons over the rough terrain and the walkers tried to keep their feet under them. Finally, the Grande Ronde Valley opened up before them, a large, lush, green valley with the river meandering through it.

On August seventh, a Sunday, the train camped at a shady, tree-covered spot along the Grande Ronde, the most perfect camping place in the world. But the valley was alive with emigrants, cattle, Indians, and ponies.

Someone said the Indians were Nez Percè and Cayuse, all friendly, well clad, and clean.

Everyone wanted to sell something, or buy or beg something. Pastor Richards gathered his flock and tried preaching but so many people and animals milling around made concentration impossible and forced him to stop. He substituted a long hymn sing that everyone enjoyed, even those coming and going.

After the service, an Indian approached Rachel, Martha, Julia, and Willie, motioning that he wanted to trade a pony. But what did he want to trade it for? He pointed at each of the girls, then the pony, who was fat, brown-and-white spotted, and pretty.

Papa came to them. "What's going on?" he asked.

"He wants to trade the pony," Rachel said, "but we can't figure what he wants to trade it for."

Looking at the Indian, Nate motioned to the pony. The Indian's eyes shifted to the girls and he pointed at Rachel, then Martha, then Julia, and back to the pony.

Nate started laughing and shook his head no. "He wants to trade it for you three girls or one of you. I'm not sure which." Nate shook his head no again, and put his arms around all three girls. "Mine," he said, pointing to the girls then himself.

The Indian nodded as if he understood, smiled a toothy grin, and walked off. Thanking Nate profusely, the girls followed him back to his wagon.

The next day they started into the Blue Mountains where thick groves of yellow pines adorned the hills, a real treat after the weeks of wallowing in the desert. But the steep hills weren't a treat for anyone, animal or man. Many of the trees carried scars from chains that the earlier emigrants used to brake the wagons on the steep descents.

The oxen began the struggle up the hills, deep moans coming from their throats, their feet so sore they stumbled on every step. Their tongues hung from the sides of their mouths and their eyes had the look of wounded animals. Every muscle of their gaunt bodies strained almost to the breaking point, trying to get the wagons up the cruel hills.

"I don't know if they can make it," Rachel said, tears streaming from her eyes.

"They'll make it," Martha choked out past her tears. "Let's pray for them."

"Dear Father in heaven, I know you love the animals more than we do," Rachel began, speaking through her tears. "I know it's a sin to force them to work so hard. But please, Father, help them do the job without injuring themselves.

"Thank you for all your mercies," Martha continued. "Could You just give them the strength to do this hard job? One more thing, Father. Please help them not to have so much pain. It's not their fault they're in such a hard place. And forgive us for abusing them. We don't know what to do. Thank You, Lord for helping us. We love You, Father. We ask these special favors in Jesus' name and thank You so much for hearing and answering our prayers."

"Amen," all their voices said together.

# fifteen

Rachel watched, hoping to see the oxen pulling easier and limping less. "I think they're better, don't you?" she asked Martha.

"Yes," Martha said, "but we still have to help them all we can." She looked down at her little brother who clung tightly to her hand. "All of us must keep praying all the time. Can you do that, Willie?" The shaggy blond head nodded.

The oxen still limped and moaned as they pulled the wagon up the hill but both Rachel and Martha thought they were doing it better.

As they neared the top of the first hill, Tom rode by on his mare. Rachel's heart beat so loudly she feared he'd hear it. "When you get to the top, wait for the men to help you," he said.

"We don't need help," Martha said. "We're doing just fine."

He laughed softly. "I'm sure you are, but we're helping all the wagons down. The hills are too steep. So just wait your turn, all right?"

The girls waited at the top even though they considered it time wasted.

When the men came, they brought a huge ox dragging a tree. "All right," Dan Barlow said. "Start your wagon down. Then stop so we can hook the tree to it."

Martha obeyed instructions. "The limbs on this tree will put a hard drag on the wagon, acting as a brake so your wagon won't run over your oxen," George Rahn said. "Just hold your animals back hard. Can you do that?"

Martha nodded; Rachel wondered if she was as sure as she acted. When the men had the tree secured to the wagon, they yelled for Martha to take the oxen down easy.

Rachel could hardly take her eyes from Tom who, with several others, grabbed the top of the pine tree, holding it back. He looked so beautiful and strong and good. How could she have ever thought he was scrawny and plain and dirty?

The wagon began descending the hill with Martha beside it talking softly to the oxen. The men pulled hard on the tree and the oxen walked slowly down the steep hill. "Stop!" someone yelled. Martha stopped the oxen until the men had everything under control. They repeated these steps several more times. A half-hour later, the wagon stood firmly at the bottom and the men led their big ox down to pull the tree back up to help the next wagon down.

They repeated the process of struggling up the hill then waiting for help to get down. "At least the oxen get to rest while we wait," Martha said.

The wagon train spent the following days going up and down hills, slowly increasing the distance from Independence, slowly nearing their new home in Oregon City.

One evening, after the train corralled, the men unyoked the oxen and led them out to feed. Rachel and Martha looked around. Majestic, dark green evergreens stood against the bright blue sky, grass grew rampantly, and a clear stream bubbled past.

Dan Barlow joined the group from somewhere with a deer draped over his horse's rump. "I have another one waiting across the ravine," he said easing the deer to the ground. In half an hour he returned with the other.

Rachel and Martha, along with the other women, washed clothes in icy water; every little while, Rachel had to warm her hands in the folds of her frock. Never in her life had she been so cold. Not only her hands but her body as well. The girls washed the Pilings' clothes, the horsemen's, and the Pitmans' though Mrs. Pitman insisted she could do it herself.

That night, the train feasted on roast meat but no one mentioned singing or dancing for a good night's sleep sounded better than anything.

The next day was Sunday, August the fourteenth. The camp at the top of the mountain caught all the early sunshine to warm the people from the cold night. After everyone enjoyed a hearty breakfast of meat, Pastor Richards led the group in a long hymn sing to warm them up then preached a sermon about the glories God is preparing for those who love Him.

"It's right to appreciate the beauty God has given us here," he said. "But it's only a shadow of things to come." As he talked about beauty, several bald eagles soared overhead, a regal sight. When he finished, he held out his hands to stop the people from leaving. "We have a special treat coming up right after this service," he said, wearing his widest smile. "I hope you'll all stay for our wagon train's first marriage. My beautiful sister, Tamara Richards, a schoolteacher, is being married to Evan Mann, a beginning attorney, and a fine man. I'm going to be proud to introduce him as my brother-in-law." He looked behind the group. "They're here now," he said, reaching his hand forward. "Come to the front, please, Tamara and Evan." He performed a simple but meaningful ceremony, ending by asking the people to all join in the Lord's Prayer.

Everyone crowded around the new couple, congratulating them and wishing them the best.

The men had put a third deer on on barbecue early that morning and soon the group enjoyed still another feast of nature's bounty in honor of the new couple. The women made biscuits to go with the meat and after Tamara and Evan were served, everyone had plenty.

Watching, Rachel could tell that Tamara wasn't entirely comfortable being the main attraction. Probably couldn't wait to get back alone. . .well, alone with her new husband.

The next day the wagon train started down the hills of the Blue Mountains for the last time. Rachel felt almost happier than she ever had.

The men still helped the wagons down and the oxen still struggled as they climbed the steep hills but each descent went a little lower. Soon, they'd be down to the prairie again.

During this time, Rachel worked so hard she barely had time to think of Tom except while he helped the wagon descend. But when she fell into her bed at night she thought of him, and dreamed of him, and prayed for him. That's all she knew to do.

They reached the valley on Saturday and camped to prepare for the Sabbath again, everyone feeling festive to be on the prairie.

The next day was Sunday, August twenty-first. The people rested, feeling they'd put in a good week's work. Rachel listened to Pastor Richards's stirring sermon with interest. He preached sermons that touched her heart every time and she had to admit he was a wonderfully dedicated man. But, she loved Tom. . .she definitely loved Tom. How could she not have known it long ago? And how could she get him to notice her?

The next day, as they descended lower into the valley, they saw majestic Mount Hood, 150 miles away. Soon, they'd pass only a few miles from that rugged, snow-capped mountain.

One day they passed a Cayuse town where the Indians raised corn, potatoes, peas, and other vegetables to sell to the travelers. Nate Butler bought some corn and potatoes and others bought what they could afford.

For the next two days, they traveled on smooth level roads, enjoying the comparatively easy traveling. Martha, Rachel, Julia, and Willie laughed, sang, told stories, and played games, something they hadn't done since before Petey died.

One day, Rachel saw a lone wagon ahead and showed Martha. "Why would it be alone out here? And with no oxen?"

Martha laughed. "I can answer that," she said. "If it weren't for your good father, I'd be sitting somewhere with just my wagon, too."

When they approached, they found a young mother with three small children, sitting on the ground beside the wagon.

Captain Ransom stopped the train. "Are you all right?" he called.

She got up and hurried to him. "No," she said. "I have a husband in the wagon who's too sick to sit up."

"Where are your animals?" Ransom asked.

"We were using oxen that belonged to a wealthy man who wouldn't let any of us ride in the wagon. When my husband got sick he took his oxen and left us here with the wagon."

"I don't know what we can do," Ransom said. "We've been picking up people all the way. I think we'll have to talk." He walked past the wagons, calling the men from them.

Rachel, who made sure she got in on most everything, couldn't think of an excuse to follow the men so she stayed with Martha.

A half-hour later, Ransom returned. "We'll try to take

you folks," he said, "but we can't take the wagon. "The Rahns will take your husband and Butler said he'll crowd you and the children into one of his wagons."

Dr. Dorland wiggled a finger at Rachel, then grabbed his medical bag. Together, they checked the family over.

"Everyone seems healthy," he said, "except the father, and I'm sure he doesn't have cholera. He'll be well in a few days."

The Ransoms gathered the small amount of food they found in the wagon and put it into their own.

When the train nooned, Papa told Mama and Rachel that he'd had to leave his blacksmith tools to take in the new family.

"How awful," Rachel said. "After you've hauled them this far."

Papa smiled sweetly. "People are more important than tools, lassie. The good Lord will provide some more tools."

The next day high winds and dust hindered the travel but they reached the Umatilla River by noon. They camped to prepare for the Sabbath and also to avoid the ill weather as much as possible.

While Rachel ate dinner with Mama and Papa, he asked her to help him a little later. "There are provisions available here," he said. "But, with all the people we've been feeding and taking into our wagons, I'll need more money." He winked at Rachel. "Could you help me get it from our bank?"

For just a second, Rachel didn't understand. Then she remembered. He'd put a big pouch of money under the false floor of one of the wagons. "I'll help you, Papa. Just call me when you're ready."

After they finished their meal, Papa told Rachel they'd pull the wagon away from the others so no one would know what they were doing. When they'd moved about a hundred feet west of the train, Papa asked Rachel to watch and tell him if anyone started toward them. Then he went to work with a screwdriver and hammer.

Rachel watched the people, listening to the many screeches and squawks as Papa pulled out the nails and lifted the false floor.

"It's gone!" Nate exclaimed. "The money's not here." After a long silence, he sighed. "I must have brought over the wrong wagon," he said. "But that floor looks as if it's been torn up before."

"You said the other wagons don't have false floors, Papa."

He nodded. Then she watched as he tore off more floorboards and double-checked to make sure the bag of money hadn't slid into a dark corner. When he looked up, his eyes met hers. She'd never seen Papa so stricken. Never, not even when she'd acted so terrible about coming.

"It's gone, Rachel," he said. "Someone took it. We're just like all the others on this train. . .almost broke."

Rachel's stomach constricted until it hurt. "Maybe you're looking in the wrong wagon," she said hopefully. "Why don't we check the others?"

He nodded. "All right, but the money's gone. Someone got it while we were away from the wagons sometime or another."

Papa checked the other wagons and found they didn't have false floors. Someone had taken the money. Almost all the money they had! "It'll be a miracle if we have enough money to get to Oregon City now," he whispered hoarsely. "Let alone having any to get started there."

"You'd better tell Captain Ransom," Rachel whispered into his ear. "What are you going to tell Mama?"

Papa looked into her eyes, his still showing shock. "I'm telling her the truth, what else?" he asked. He motioned for her to follow. “Come, let’s tell Ransom.”

The grizzly haired and whiskered man stood in silence after Nate explained what had happened. “I don’t rightly know what to do,” the kind captain said. “We both know you’ll never see that money again.” He looked off into the blue sky. “We don’t even know whether it was our own people or someone else,” he mused.

“Whoever took it knew it was there,” Rachel said. “We haven’t been away from the wagon long at any time. Someone had to go right to the spot and get the money in a hurry.”

Ransom nodded. “Right. It was a slick one. Want me to try to bluff the guilty man into giving it back? I’m afraid that kind don’t bluff.”

As they walked back to their wagons, Rachel felt devastated. No doubt about it, this was Heartbreak Trail. NO! Money lacked a lot of being everything. God saw the person steal the money and allowed it. Why? Maybe the person’s family was starving. Maybe the Butler family would grow closer to God without money. Maybe God had some special blessing in store for them. Maybe He just allowed this to happen for no special reason. But Rachel didn’t believe that for a minute. God loved her family much more than they loved each other so there was a purpose in all this. And they’d be all right.

She dropped back and walked beside Papa. “It’s all right, Papa,” she said softly. “God just showed me we’ll be all right.”

Nate reached an arm down, dropped it over her shoulder, and smiled. “Know what, lassie?” he asked. “He just showed me the same thing. He’ll care for our needs.”

Then it was Sunday, August thirty-first. Indians roamed back and forth, Pastor Richards started his hymn sing, and many of the Indians joined them. After the singing,

Pastor Richards preached a basic sermon about God's love and sacrifice for all.

"Thank Him for loving you so much," he told them, "and tell Him you love Him, too, and want to belong to Him. He'll come right into your heart and live with you forever."

Rachel watched the Indians and prayed for them as they listened with rapt attention.

That afternoon, when Rachel took food to the Piling family, she found Tom there. "What are you doing?" she asked.

He grinned as he turned pink. "I'm cooking," he said. "Remember I said I would?" Rachel remembered, but she hadn't taken it seriously. Setting her food down, she helped him finish the meal. Serving it onto plates, they gave one to Sandra for her and Judith, and handed one to Mr. Piling.

Piling took the food but didn't thank them for it or speak. He just glowered at them as if they'd intruded.

Rachel felt surprised when his rudeness didn't upset her. She didn't feel hurt or mad. Nothing. Just concern for Sandy and her baby. Thank You, Lord. You're changing me from a self-centered hothead into a human being. Thank You again, God. I love You.

"Does he always treat you like this?" she whispered to Tom.

Tom nodded. "He's pretty good today. Must be because you're here. Let's clean up and get out of here."

"Is Martha still going to Walla Walla Valley?" he asked on the way back.

Rachel nodded. "I can't bear it, Tom. I just can't let her go. Help me talk to her, will you?"

He grinned and nodded. "Sure. But she won't listen to me. You're her closest friend."

"I've said all the words I know. She won't listen."

Again, Rachel begged Martha to go to Oregon City but she wouldn't consider it. "My family will be looking for me," she said, her usual reply.

The next day Nate prepared to take one of his wagons to Walla Walla Valley to leave with Martha but bring back the oxen he'd lent her. "Try once more to talk her into going on with us," he told Rachel and Rachel begged her not to go. While Rachel was begging, Rachel's mother, Alma, came up. "If you go," she said in a soft loving voice, "I can't let Willie leave with you."

"He has to come with me," Martha cried. "He and Josie are all I have. He has to stay with me."

"How much food do you have?" Alma asked kindly.

"Almost none," Martha admitted. "Just a pint of flour. But my family will be in the Walla Walla Valley nearly as soon as I will."

Tom had arrived and stood beside Rachel. "We can't know that, Martha," he said. "They may not come until spring. Or not at all. We aren't even sure they ever started, are we?"

Martha stared at him with wide eyes. "They planned to come within a week after we left."

Alma wrapped Martha in her arms and held her tightly. "Please, stay with us. You might starve to death if you go."

Martha shook her dark head. "I purely have to go, Mrs. Butler. My aunt and uncle and my cousin and brother will be there. What will they do if I'm not there?"

"But they have each other," Tom said. "You're going to be all alone."

Martha looked serious. A dull red rimmed her eyes. "I have to go."

Alma nodded. "We'll give you a gallon of flour. That's all we dare let go of now that we don't have money. We're taking Willie. Either you can come after him or we'll bring him back next spring."

Martha didn't argue, but dropped her head in defeat.

Julia hugged Martha tightly but couldn't talk. Dan Barlow, standing nearby, put his arm around Julia. "Now, don't you be worrying about Miss Tate," he told Martha. "I plan to keep her safe. And happy, too. So you just take care of yourself and Josie."

Pastor Richards made a passionate plea for Martha to go on with them to Oregon City, insinuating he'd make sure she was cared for. She shook her head.

The other Butler wagons would rest at the Umatilla River until the Butlers returned. Captain Ransom hadn't decided whether the train would wait or continue on.

Right after nooning, Martha led her oxen off toward Walla Walla Valley. Rachel walked with Martha and Papa drove their oxen. The sun shone brightly, prairie grass, though half-dried, grew everywhere.

On the second day they met some Indians with lots of potatoes and wanting to trade. Nate traded one of his shirts for a dozen nice big potatoes. Before the sun set, they reached their destination, Steptoeville, in Walla Walla Valley.

As they approached, only a few, eight to be exact, rough buildings, four on each side of a Nez Percè trail, met their eyes. Several dirty tepees huddled on the north side of the trail behind the shacks.

About a quarter-mile away, past the rickety buildings, a group of even smaller and more destitute shacks sprawled, obviously deserted.

"Doesn't look much like the Garden of Eden to me," Rachel said. "Oh, Martha, I'm sorry. Please, come with us to Oregon City."

# sixteen

Martha laughed shakily. "You're purely right, Rachel. It doesn't look as beautiful as I expected." Then she pointed south and east. "But look at the mountains. They're pretty enough."

Nate looked, too. "Say," he said, "I think those are the Blue Mountains. We just came over some of them."

The little group parked the wagon at the west end of the Indian trail and unyoked the oxen. A small stream to the north provided plenty of water for the animals as they began grazing on the grass.

The girls prepared a meal with the potatoes, side meat, and biscuits, a feast fit for kings, Rachel said.

On Sunday, September eleventh, Rachel and Martha decided this was the quiet Sabbath for which they had been waiting. Entirely too quiet, they agreed before the day ended. Rachel and Papa spent the entire day trying to talk Martha into going back with them but she couldn't be persuaded.

Early the next morning, Papa gave Martha two of the remaining four potatoes and yoked up the oxen. Rachel's heart hurt so badly she couldn't talk, not even to beg Martha once more to come.

As they returned the way they'd come, Rachel looked back to see Martha kneeling beside Josie, hugging the dog tightly, and waving as hard as she could.

Rachel sobbed until she could barely walk. She ended up crying all the way back. Would she ever again see her dearest friend in the world? Her friend who taught her to love and serve Jesus. Her friend who taught her how to love and be kind. Please be with Martha, she cried silently. Take good care of her, Father. She has no money and so little food. Send someone to help her right away. Oh, thank You, God. I love You so much.

When they reached the Umatilla River again, they discovered the wagon train had gone on. But two of the horse riders and Tom had waited. Now they had three wagons and about a dozen people in their group.

As Tom ran to greet Rachel, her first thought was of her eyes, red from crying. When Tom reached her, he stopped and Rachel could see the struggle in his mind. He wanted to hug her! She knew he did.

His arms moved nervously as he stepped from one foot to the other. Finally, he forced himself to settle down. "Welcome back!" he said heartily. "We missed you a lot."

Rachel swallowed. In her wildest dreams she hadn't expected Tom to show this much enthusiasm for her return. "Thank you," she said. "Your welcome makes me feel better. It hurt me so much to leave Martha in that desolate place."

Willie spotted Rachel and came running to her. "Where's Martha?" he asked, tugging on her long calico skirt. "I want Martha now."

Rachel knelt and hugged the little boy. "Martha couldn't come right now," she said, holding him close. "She asked me to take care of you until she can have you with her. She loves you a lot, Willie, and will come after you as soon as she can. Can you be happy with us until then?"

He nodded and returned her hug. Poor little boy. First, he lost his parents, then his brother, next his best friend, and now his sister. Rachel gave him an extra tight hug. She'd have to be mother, father, sister, and friend to Willie while he was with them.

The next few days Rachel tried hard to keep Willie happy. She had nothing else to do or anyone else to be with so she didn't mind. Rather, she enjoyed his company as they walked, sang Jesus songs, and played games.

The small company camped early on Saturday to prepare for the Sabbath. After Rachel and Mama did the wash for everyone, they made a pie with the last of the dried apples. "At least we'll have a decent Sabbath," Mama said.

On Sunday, September twenty-fifth, the sun shone brightly even though October would soon be upon them. The whole group ate together since the Butlers were the only ones with wagons and cooking things.

Since there was no preacher, Tom led the group in a hymn sing. The dozen people made a joyful noise unto the Lord. In fact, Rachel thought they sounded all right. After the singing, Nate read some praise chapters from Psalms.

Later, after lunch, Tom asked Rachel to walk with him. He lead her to a quiet place, overlooking the valley.

"Beautiful," Rachel said. "This looks a lot more like the Garden of Eden than where Martha is."

"You may not have seen the best of the Walla Walla Valley," he said.

She laughed softly. "I hope not. What I saw wasn't very nice. But you know what? I asked God to send someone to help her right away, and I know He did. I have His peace to assure me. It makes all the difference."

"You've changed a lot since we started on the Trail," he said quietly. "Do you realize that?"

She nodded. "Yes. That's because God found me, even on Heartbreak Trail. He's with us no matter where we go, did you know that? No matter how foolish we are or what dumb things we do, He's there to help us. Isn't that remarkable? If I were God, I wouldn't be that good."

He laughed. "You would, Rachel, because you'd be God. Perfect, long-suffering, complete love. I've learned to appreciate you a lot on this long painful trip. You've been irreplaceable, helping with my work. I can't thank you enough for that."

"I enjoyed it, Tom. A lot. You may be right, saying I should be a nurse."

"I don't want to lose you, Rachel. I want you to go on helping me."

"I will. If you stay around. I'd really enjoy that." Rachel giggled. "I purely would, as Martha would say."

Tom swallowed loudly. "I didn't exactly mean just with my medicine," he said in a choked voice. "I've loved you for a long time, Rachel. I want to marry you when we catch up with Pastor Richards. . .or another preacher."

Rachel couldn't answer. Were her dreams coming true? Out here, on Heartbreak Trail? Where she'd seen nothing but death and disaster? She tried to swallow the lump in her throat. Then she sniffled.

"Is there someone else?" he asked quietly. "Maybe back in Quincy?"

She swallowed again. And sniffed again. "No," she whimpered. "I've never loved anyone but you. Never. I've loved you for a long time, too. Why didn't you tell me sooner?"

He smiled tenderly. "Well, I noticed you the first thing. I'd never seen such beautiful hair in my life. And your eyes, Rachel. They're something to take away a man's breath. You caught my attention right away but," his eyes twinkled, "somehow I got the idea you were spoiled. And that you didn't care all that much about God. The life I have to offer a woman will be hard; I need a woman with lots of faith, one who isn't afraid to work."

Rachel laughed into his eyes. "So, I wasn't good enough for you."

He shook his sunshiny hair. "No, you just weren't right for me. But I couldn't quit watching you, and admiring you from a distance. And I ended up watching you grow."

They talked a while then ambled back to the wagons where they found Nate.

"I have something important to ask you," Tom said. Rachel could see concern in Tom's eyes.

"Well, sit here on the wagon's tongue," Nate said. "I'll do my best to give you a good answer."

Tom stood. "Rachel and I have just discovered we love each other," he began.

Alma burst into laughter. "Why didn't you ask me? I could have told you a long time ago."

Tom smiled. "Well, we learned that we've cared for each other for some time, all right." He turned his attention back to Nate. "I'm asking for your blessing, sir, as I'd like nothing more than to marry Rachel and spend my life caring for her and making her happy."

Nate jumped up from the wagon hitch he'd been sitting on and extended his hand to Tom. "Welcome, Tom," he said happily. "I can't say this is a complete surprise. Not with Alma whispering in my ear. But you're exactly like the son I never had. I'd be honored to have you marry my only daughter."

Alma rushed out and hugged Tom. "Willie, can you give Tom a hug, too?" she asked when she released him. "He's going to be even more special to us now." Willie hugged Tom, always glad to get another hug.

After everyone quieted, Tom asked Rachel to walk with him again. When they found the same quiet place, Tom pulled her into his arms. "Everyone's been hugging but us," he whispered into her hair. "I love you my flaming-haired princess and want to never be separated from you again, not even for one day." His arm gently circled her waist as he pulled her closer, tipped up her face, and kissed her parted lips ever so gently.

Rachel returned the kiss that sent tremors through her entire body. A moment later she pulled away, discovering she'd never felt so lightheaded in her life. . .or so happy. She pulled his lips back to hers. "I'm dizzy," she whispered, "but kiss me again. I love you an awful lot."

The next day they traveled on, Rachel walking with Willie. She tried to sing all the songs and play all the games Martha had. The little boy seemed happy but he clung to her with quiet desperation.

Tom came around several times each day and every night he helped Rachel clean up after the meal. Then they walked and talked and dreamed.

One day at noon they reached the mighty Columbia River. Standing on the banks of the river she'd read about, sang about, and heard about all her life, Rachel felt small and insignificant. What was she? A fly compared to this river, and even less compared to the universe God had created. How could He care about anything so small as her? Oh, but I'm glad You do, Lord. Thank You for loving me, even more than the mighty things You've made. Thank You, Lord. I love You, too."

The group nooned on the bank of the river and traded some old clothes to Indians for a huge salmon, then headed for the Deschutes River where they camped.

On October first, Rachel and Tom spent the cold and rainy day together in one of the Butler wagons with her folks, making plans and trying to keep warm.

The next day they reached The Dalles, 1820 miles from Independence, about one hundred miles from Oregon City. The Dalles was almost the climax of the journey, the place where they had to decide whether to go by boat on the river or to take the Barlow Road over the Cascade Mountains. The Cascades were said to be even steeper and more dangerous than the Blue Mountains.

Rachel felt disappointed in The Dalles. She'd hoped she'd finally reach civilization there, but the town consisted of only a few houses; she'd call them shacks.

"I know we need food," Papa said as they walked around a little, "but I have to find out how much it's going to cost us to get over the Cascades before I spend anything."

Nate, Tom, and Rachel walked down to the docks where boats constantly loaded for the trip downriver. A man, obviously a traveler, spoke to them.

"Howdy," Nate said. "We're wondering what's the best way to get to Oregon City."

The man laughed out loud. "You and everyone else," he said. "Well, I'll tell you the best way. Put everthin' you got on boats, even your livestock. 'Course, I can't afford that so I'm tearin' up my wagon, an' shippin' it and all my goods and my wimmin folks. Me and my hired man're gonna drive the cattle over Barlow Road." He shook his head, sending his wild gray hair into a worse mess than before. "By the time the cattle git here they ain't got the stren'th to walk over, let alone haul wagons over."

Nate asked how much it cost to send a wagon and goods. Satisfied by the man's response, he smiled and extended his hand. "That's just what I'm going to do, too. Sounds like a good compromise."

The man shook Nate's hand aggressively. "Best bet," he said. "But if yore gonna go over the Road, best not to even ride yore horses. I heerd of several good saddle horses not making it neither. Just lead the horses and don't push none of the stock."

Nate thanked the man again and headed for the shipping office where he booked passage for three wagons, the contents, and two women.

"I'm not going by boat, Papa," Rachel said. "Tom will take care of me if I walk. Who'll help us when the boat sinks?"

Alma seconded the motion so they all worked together to get the wagons and barrels of goods ready to ship, then planned their own trip over the Cascades.

"We can buy some food now," Nate said. "Let's find some."

Before they found any food they stumbled across an overgrown potato patch. "Looks as if no one plans to dig these spuds," Tom said. "Why don't we check on them?"

When they found the owner, he said he hadn't planned to dig them. "If you'll do the work, I'll let 'em go for five dollars a hunnert."

"I don't think we can haul them over the mountains," Alma told Nate.

"Why couldn't we divide them among all the horses?" Tom asked. "Potatoes sound good about now."

They dug two hundred pounds of the potatoes and decided they'd better stop before they had the animals loaded too heavily.

"Are we going to buy other things to eat?" Rachel asked.

Nate shook his head. "Someone might shoot something. Otherwise, we'll eat potatoes until we reach Oregon City." He gave her a quick squeeze. "Things are different for us since we lost our money, lassie."

"Potatoes will be fine," Rachel said. The others agreed so they packed the saddlebags with potatoes, a big skillet, side meat grease, dishes, and silver, and started over the mountains.

The road seemed to be mostly cleared of trees and the biggest rocks, but the ascents and descents were even steeper than those in the Blue Mountains.

"I'm so thankful the animals aren't pulling wagons," Rachel said.

"So am I," Tom, who was walking with her, said. "And I for one will try to keep anyone from pushing the animals." He looked up the hill beside the road where the trees grew so closely together that a man would have trouble walking between them. "Do you realize the first people over had to clear away trees as they went?"

Rachel prayed silently for God to help them all, people and animals, over the brutal road. Carcasses of oxen, cows, and horses lay at the edge, testifying starkly to the still unmerciful road.

"I'm thankful to God for being so good to us so far," Nate said. "Do you realize we still have all of our original animals plus the one that joined our herd?" His eyes turned soft as he looked at Rachel. "Mama and I talked last night and decided to give half our animals to you and Tom when we reach Oregon City. That's half of thirteen cows, three saddle horses, and thirty oxen."

Rachel hugged her father, then her mother. "Thank you both. That's enough for a good start. We'll take good care of them as you have."

That night Alma and Rachel fried enough potatoes to fill up all the people traveling with them. Everyone enjoyed the change the potatoes brought.

For the next two days the weather stayed warm and dry though the evenings turned downright cold. The group slept, wrapped in blankets, under the stars.

One of the young men went ahead and brought back

some rabbits to go with the fried potatoes. They all agreed they were eating like kings.

Then it clouded up and rained. Everyone got soaked and so did their blankets. Fortunately, lots of tree branches lay near the edge of the road so that night they made a roaring fire and tried to dry their clothes and blankets.

"It's hard," Rachel complained. "The fire's so hot I can't stand close enough to dry the blankets." The blankets finally dried but as soon as they put them on the ground the wet seeped into them again.

The next morning Rachel got up, sore and chilled, to help Mama cook potatoes again.

When they started walking, the road was wet and slippery; the animals picked their way carefully. The oxen and horses, shod, fared better than the loose cattle.

Tom and Rachel walked carefully, each leading a horse. Rachel felt tired before nooning time and couldn't wait for the rest. As the group struggled up the hill, Tom's horse's foot struck a slick rock and slipped, knocking Tom's feet out from under him.

Although quick, Tom couldn't catch his balance. He fell to the ground, hitting his head on a sharp stone and cutting his forehead. Blood gushed from the wound as Tom lay dazed, uncaring.

# seventeen

"Grab something and shove it against the wound!" Mama yelled.

Rachel snatched the hem of her skirt, turned the worst mud inside, folded the fabric a few times, and shoved it into the jagged cut in his forehead.

Tom stirred and opened his eyes. "I'm all right," he said, evidently reading fear in the faces gathered around him. "Head wounds bleed profusely." He looked at Rachel, kneeling next to him and still pressing the hem of her skirt into the wound. "You'll have to sew it up, Rachel."

An enormous lump dropped into her stomach. She couldn't do that! She shook her head. "I'll hold my skirt against it all day but I can't sew you up. You know I can't, Tom."

He grinned, emphasizing his white face. "Sure you can. You've watched me enough times."

"I can't, Tom." How could he ask her to do something like that, anyway? He'd gone to school a long time to learn how to be a doctor. Now he expected her to be one with no training at all! Then she noticed blood oozing through the skirt she held against his head. "Are you going to bleed to death?" she whispered.

He smiled wearily. "No, I won't bleed to death. But if you don't stitch it up, I'll have a bad scar. Looking at my face will scare you so much you'll run away and refuse to marry me."

She shook her head. It finally sank into her head that

Tom couldn't sew up his own wound. None of this group knew anything about medicine. Almost for sure she knew more than any of the others after having helped Tom for the last six months. "Will you tell me what to do?" she whimpered.

A look of relief crossed his face. "Exactly," he said. "Get my bag off my horse." She did. "Now, find the pouch that says needle and thread. Put the thread through the needle just as if you were going to do some embroidery. Then, pour some of the whiskey over it."

Rachel did everything he told her, feeling shaky with all the eyes watching. After pouring whiskey over the needle and thread, she knew the next step—cleaning his wound. She held up the bottle and showed Tom.

He nodded, giving her a small smile. "I get to find out how it feels, don't I?"

She turned his head so the whiskey wouldn't run into his eyes, then slowly poured it across the wound. Watching his arm and neck muscles tighten, she knew it hurt. "I'm sorry," she whispered and touched his lips with hers before remembering the dozen people watching.

His arms reached gently around her, pulling her closer. "Thanks," he whispered against her lips. "That helped a lot." Then he lay back on the ground again sighing. "I guess I'm not very strong right now," he said. "Better get me fixed up."

"All right, Tom, but you have to help me."

With his eyes closed, he instructed her. "Close the wound with your left hand," he said almost in a whisper, "and stitch with the other. Be sure to get the thread through all the layers of the skin."

A picture appeared in Rachel's mind of Tom working on Josie, so much more horrible. She saw him bringing the skin together over the dog's intestines, pushing the needle through the thick layer of skin, then pulling the skin together and stitching again.

She knew exactly how to do it. But it would hurt him! No matter, it had to be done. "All right," she said softly. "Relax. I can do it." She followed the picture in her mind, step by step, until she put the last stitch in and secured the thread.

Tom hadn't said a word and barely flinched while she worked.

"I'm all through," she said when he didn't stir. She leaned down to his ear. "Know what happened?" she asked, then answered her own question. "I did a perfect job," she said. "God showed me how to do it, step by step. In pictures, Tom. He showed me in pictures."

Tom opened his eyes but obviously didn't share her enthusiasm at that point. "Good girl. I knew He would." He quieted and rested a few minutes then opened his eyes and found Rachel again. "Know why He showed you?" he asked.

Rachel nodded, her eyes dewy from the strain but still thrilled with what had happened. "Because you needed help and there wasn't anyone else."

He nodded, his eyes closed. "That, too," he agreed quietly. "But He showed you because you're walking that close to Him now. If you weren't, you wouldn't have heard Him."

Papa built a big fire and Mama cooked up several more skillets of potatoes, which everyone ate with relish—except Tom who didn't feel hungry.

"I wish you could eat," Rachel told him, sitting close. "I'm hungrier than I've ever been in my life." She giggled. "I didn't realize how much energy it takes to sew people up."

By evening Tom ate like a hungry ranch hand and by

the next morning he walked as well as any of the little company.

Sunday, October ninth, was cloudy and dry but not too cold. So, Tom led the small company of believers in all the songs they could remember. When they finished, Nate read some Psalms then offered a prayer of praise and thanksgiving for caring for them on the long hard trip and bringing them safely to God's Garden of Eden on earth.

When he started to dismiss them, Rachel stopped him. "I have something to say," she said, running to the front. "I just wanted to tell you something God did for me," she said, facing the group breathlessly. "I'd helped Tom sew up several animals and people but I didn't remember how to do it. But when I started to sew Tom's wound, God showed me, step by step, how to do it. He did such a fine job that the wound is looking good already and Tom isn't in pain. It made me think of something He wants to do for us. If we'll read the Bible faithfully, He'll bring it to our minds when we need it. Isn't that fantastic?"

Several people said, "Amen" or "Yes, Lord."

Suddenly, Rachel didn't know what to say. "I guess that's all," she finally said. "I just thought it was so special I wanted to share it."

Nate Butler started them early the next morning as all were getting excited about arriving in Oregon City. No one knew exactly when it would be but they all knew it would be soon. . .very soon.

Two days later, they reached the summit. A rough sign stated the fact in black hand-painted letters, surely one of the most beautiful sights Rachel had ever seen.

That night the group celebrated with a small deer one of the men had shot. They built a spit, placing a strong green log over two crossed logs and hung the cleaned animal by its hooves until it turned brown with juices oozing out all over the carcass. The meat and potatoes made a meal they all ate with relish.

The next morning they started down the rugged mountains.

"Down is always easier than up, isn't it?" Rachel asked Tom.

He grinned. "Always," he agreed, "unless there's a wagon behind the animals trying to run over them. Then I'm not sure."

As he talked, Rachel noticed how well his forehead was healing. Not a bit of redness remained, the swelling had gone from the wound, and it looked almost insignificant. Rachel touched the spot. "How does it feel now?" she asked.

He snatched her to him. "You look beautiful, like my own healing angel, like my dearest gift from God, like my reason for living." He released her and looked into her eyes. "That was what you asked, wasn't it?"

She shook her head, laughing into his eyes. "I asked how your wound. . .you know what I asked. So tell me."

"It's all well. I've kept track of it with my fingers. It's smooth, no puffiness or drawing at the stitches. Nothing. It isn't even sore anymore." He stopped and looked to his left, then to his right. "Don't let the word get around, though. I'll lose all my patients to my associate. . .," his eyes softened as they looked into hers, "my wife," he finished. "One of these days I'll be asking my doctor to remove the stitches."

Alarm bolted through her chest, then quieted. "That's easy, isn't it?"

He nodded. "Simple as pulling a tree down a mountain." Then he laughed. "Yes, it's easy. It'll take about five minutes with no pain or strain."

Nate kept the group moving slowly, though all, even the animals, were eager to reach the bottom of the mountain. "We don't need any accidents now," he said. "So far we're all still here, man and animal alike. But just think how close we came to losing one of us. If Tom had broken a leg we'd have had to shoot him."

As they traveled, Rachel kept her eyes west. Sometime soon the mountains would drop behind them and Oregon City would spread out before them. "What do you think it'll look like?" she asked Tom. "Will it be a nice, thriving city?"

Tom shook his head. "I think it'll look pretty primitive. Some log cabins, a few rough stores. I think there'll be lots of farming and cattle but nothing you'd consider a city."

She clung to his arm. "I can't wait to get there." Her eyes rose to his. "Know why?"

He smiled, his eyes filled with love. "No, but I know why I'm eager."

"Is it so we can find a minister?" she asked softly.

"You guessed it the first time," he said with joy. "You can't know how happy I am that you didn't say you wanted some big department stores or fancy restaurants."

She laughed, a happy sound that gladdened all hearts that heard it. Her eyes twinkled with mischief. "I'm sure some great stores and restaurants would have been my first wish if someone hadn't taken all our money. Now I have to settle for you, Dr. Thomas Dorland." She laughed again. "What a letdown."

All that day they came down hills then went back up, though not as far up as down. The entire group was caught up in a sort of holiday atmosphere for their destination lay almost within their grasp and that was reason enough to be excited.

When they started the next day, Rachel knew for sure that it would be the day but no Oregon City popped into view between the mountains and they had to camp one more night on the road.

"I just checked the animals," Tom said, later that night. "They're surprisingly well considering what they've been through. No doubt they'll all make it now.

Late the next afternoon, Rachel thought the mountains were beginning to thin out. But, once again, they camped under the stars, cold but dry stars.

The next day, Rachel and Tom talked so much and so fast that someone else spotted the city before she did.

"There she is!" someone yelled at the top of his voice. "Laid out like a picture between them mountains."

The beautiful sight, plus the thrill of seeing the end of their journey, wrenched Rachel's breath from her throat. A huge valley lay beyond the craggy mountains. White frame houses, each surrounded by acres and acres of farmland, barns, and corrals looked exactly like Rachel had hoped.

Nate pulled the Mormon guidebook from his pocket. "This thing says we're one thousand, nine hundred thirty miles from Independence."

"Does it say we're five miles from our new home, the Garden of Eden?" Rachel asked.

He shook his head, joy displayed over his face. "No, but that's about it."

No one wanted to stop for nooning, so they continued on. The descent leveled out soon and the highly excited little company walked as if they'd just begun the long trek rather than ending it.

Rachel felt so much joy she didn't know if she could contain it. Here, before her, was her new home. . .her new home with her new husband. She thanked God that

He'd impressed Papa to force her to come on Heartbreak Trail.

It had taken a lot for God to get her attention. Maybe she'd have never come to know Him if she'd stayed in Quincy where everything always went right. Sometimes it takes pain to draw people to Him. Heartbreak Trail had done it for Rachel. How could she have ever gotten along for so long without her dear heavenly Father?

She'd wanted to stay in Quincy to find the cream of the crop, but God had the very very best waiting for her on the wagon train. And when she was ready, He brought Tom to her. Not when she acted like a baby, but when she grew up!

*Thank You, God. Please take charge of my life forever. I love You!*